RAGE OF AQUARIUS

A CATE CONWAY MYSTERY

COLLEEN MACLEOD

Cover Photo: Morgan Lake, La Grande, Oregon
© Rod Koopman

ISBN: 1-4392-2390-4
ISBN-13: 9781439223901

Visit www.booksurge.com to order additional copies.

*To Emma Alta Kirk Chilson, my grandmother
and Lillian Geraldine Chilson Conway, my
mother; both long past, who still sit at my shoulder
and give me words.*

*For Alan Ross MacLeod, my husband,
who crafts songs so beautiful, they make me weep.*

✬✬✬

*and to Hoover and Spooter two remarkably
human cow dogs.*

CHAPTER ONE

On an over-warm, spring afternoon I climbed the steps of the old hotel annex with mid-day weariness. The elevator was still closed for upgrades. If that meant that it would, in future, align more directly with the floor to which it was destined, then I was delighted with the inconvenience. It was always alarming to have to crawl up out of the elevator cage onto the landings.

The office was four floors up and cramped like an old hotel room. That was exactly what it had been until the late fifties, when the old hotel annex had fallen into poor repair and even poorer management. The new owners had been slowly remodeling, or 'de-modeling' as they liked to call it. They sought to capture the feel of the thirties and forties when the old landmark had been in its heyday. That was back when the ballroom in the old Sacajawea Hotel next door had sparkled with the surrounding area's society. The bathroom was down the carpet-runnered hall, and I shared those facilities jointly with the floor's three other current inhabitants. Not the executive suite, nor did the annex even offer that possibility, but it was absolutely perfect for me. It kept my office separate from my house and it also kept me from bringing what some might consider unsavory clients into my home.

My business, Conway Investigations, inhabited the room that faced the sporadically working elevator doors. To the right of me was a graphic artist, who claimed that she reached the most opportune 'right brain efficiency' to the accompaniment of Wagner. This brought those rather loud, German, funereal strains through the walls at times and they became a murky cacophony when mixed with the inaccurate music scales being practiced in the piano teacher's studio, which occupied the space to my direct left. An accountant shared the next space to the left, leaving six other empty offices on the floor, all awaiting future *de-modeling*.

I regularly blessed the delay of their completion.

As I elbowed open the stairwell door and stepped into the cool comfort of the hallway, my eye caught the white envelope taped to the door of my office. It covered a corner of the black-edged, gold paint that announced **CONWAY INVESTIGATIONS,** and the motto beneath, *"There's a right way, a wrong way and a Conway"*. It was an old saying of my father's and it seemed to fit the gray areas that I found myself maneuvering through in the course of seeking out life's little secrets. It explained the occasional bending of rules and unorthodox methods that investigative work sometimes required.

I pulled the envelope off and keyed open my door. The old skeleton key stood out among the short, boxey modern ones on my key ring. I often found myself absently rubbing its worn smoothness and wondered how many hands had held it over the years. One might wonder how secure an office door might be with this old lock system, but that had never worried me too much. A skeleton key was no protection against theft, but I knew from personal experience that an intruder who wanted entry badly enough could get past deadbolts with proper motivation.

I counted on the all too often fourth floor hike to my office to be as much of a deterrent as any chains or bolts.

Even in my line of work, which did occasionally illuminate life's seamier side, I considered my small

Oregon town a quiet haven, generally much safer than the larger cities in the state. La Grande is a relatively quiet eastern Oregon town, twelve and a half thousand people, and we do have a share of police blotter action; all of which is published, historically, six afternoons a week in the town's newspaper, The Observer.

I set the envelope down on my desk along with my too-large purse and the weight of the bag swept a few no-fee credit card offers and unread grocery circulars closer to their eventual destination, the recycle box on the floor. It had been weeks since I had made a rubbish run, or dusted, or filed and the small space was starting to close in. I mentally promised myself an all day run at straightening on Saturday.

I punched the replay button on my answering machine and collapsed on the elderly, blue, overstuffed couch by the window in order to rub aching calf muscles. The machine had the annoying habit of always replaying my recorded message before divulging its contents, so, I sat through the canned version of me saying, *"Conway Investigations, This is Cate Conway. I am not available right now, but if you leave a name or number and the time you called, I do check my messages several times a day and I will return your call."*

I had learned long ago that the majority of my callers might not wish to leave a permanent recording regarding the nature of their business or their desired service on my tape. I had stopped asking for particulars. The devil was in the details and the devil is generally best spoken of privately and face to face.

The Cate is for Catriona, pronounced Katreena. It is a paternal family name, very Gaelic, hard to pronounce and was a reflection of my father's penchant for all that was Irish, Catholic or fermented. It is only one of the burdens he shouldered me with. From grade school on I have been Cate and have only had to correct the 'C' not 'K' spelling aspect of it practically every time it has ever been written.

Today's messages revealed I had forgotten an appointment with Dr. Spencer, my dentist, my sister had secured hotel reservations for our annual 'summer sister getaway' and my treasured old four wheel drive pickup, Sam, was done at the shop, the final repairs totaling only $675.98.

I could survive in the wilderness for extended periods of time, repair assorted small electrical appliances with some success and even cook gourmet without recipes, but the workings of an internal combustion engine are a foreign language that escape my comprehension. Therefore, I was at the mercy of any repairman who insisted my gizmo oscillator was malfunctioning.

I merely believed, and paid.

Considering the vintage on my 1959 Ford, repairs were a given, but it had been the last vehicle my grandfather ever bought and I continued to baby it with all the love and affection with which he had honored it.

I called the truck Sam, after that grandfather. I had recently had it repainted in the same bright red color that had caught my granddaddy's eye and had so mortified my grandmother. Not an unobtrusive vehicle for stakeouts, but it was one hundred percent me.

I had a particularly solid bond with those maternal grandparents, having spent a large portion of every childhood summer with them. Given the storm clouds that darkened my own parent's relationship, those summer months were respite care, which I looked forward to through the winter of my parent's discontent. My father had unresolved issues with parental abandonment and that led to an Irish fondness for alcohol and severely underdeveloped parental skills.

My mother, unable to stand up to the whirlwind that was her husband, tried in her own quiet way to insulate her children from his drunken, manic, abusive mood swings. She had married young and had always been a traditional homemaker. She came from an era where that had been expected. It created in her adult life, a lack of self-esteem, as she felt she possessed no real marketable job skills. For too many years it prevented her escape and trapped her family as well.

She finally left him when I was grown, but not until she had found another man to care for her. She was somewhat more successful with that choice, although, by that time, I was past needing a father to bond with and he and I never really connected.

I have two brothers and a sister. All three of them live at least a days drive away. Growing up, we created an insular little 'family within a family' that has continued into our adult lives. As the offspring of an alcoholic, we developed a series of silent gestures and communication that could sound the alarm; such as ' dad is half through a bottle and he is looking for a fight-don't start anything, escape to the tree fort- we'll talk there'. Several of those same gestures I use to this day when I am training Hoover my partner dog.

Danger comes in all forms and sometimes you can't shout out verbal warnings.

We three remain a combination of parent-sibling to each other that may be common with children who lived through the thrills and spills of Johnnie Walker's wild carnival ride.

We get together infrequently, which actually keeps our bond stronger. Families can be like a delicious slice of cheesecake. Best when enjoyed in small pieces. You can revel in the richness, admire the texture but too large a slice and you end up pushing it away, feeling slightly uncomfortable and leaving some behind on your plate.

My parents are both gone now. I think I've gotten over most of the resentments long ago, and as they say, that which doesn't kill you makes you strong. Someone pointed out once that if you are going to blame your parents for how bad things are with you, you have to give them equally the credit for all of the good.

Fair enough. What's good or bad about me, I choose to take credit for.

I think I am pretty tough because of it all. Part of my learned, life skills are an aversion to alcohol. I do not drink, which actually makes a lot of sense in my business situations. I generally tend to avoid entanglements with anyone who appears to have problems with the demon rum. I certainly don't have the problem of needing to find a man 'just like the one that married dear old mom', but I don't avoid relationships for fear of making my mother's same mistakes.

I may be a trifle independent, which has ruffled up a couple of relationships, but I am convinced everyone needs the ability to completely care for themselves, and any fellow who feels threatened by an independent woman will be guaranteed trouble down the road.

I don't think I have taken up a traditionally masculine profession to compensate for my mother's insecurities or my father's abuses, but who needs psychoanalysis when a nice trip to the gun range, with a leprechaun shaped target, is rewarding enough.

I stood up and retrieved the white envelope from my desk and turned it over to run my finger under the glued flap. I half expected a note from the building owners announcing some new renovation delay.

That was not the case.

Inside was a folded newspaper article and directions to someplace outside of Union, a smaller community about fifteen miles to the southeast of La Grande. The clipping was age-yellowed. There was no date, nor banner to announce it's source, but the by-line was La Grande. The newspaper had recently celebrated its 100th birthday, so it was safe to venture that the source was either the *Observer*, its predecessor *The Evening Observer,* or one of the competitive rags that had fought for and lost news dominance in the area. It reported the disappearance and suspected abduction of a prominent young woman on the night of May 21. Police had brought in, and questioned a few acquaintances of Mary Milton, but had been unable to find a clue as to her disappearance or exactly when she had gone missing from her parent's south hill home. Her father, a local physician, had posted a reward and the usual details followed; a description of the girl, clothing that she was last seen wearing and a plea for anyone's related knowledge.

I laid down the clipping and studied the map. It was to an area up Catherine Creek, outside of Union. It was where this part of rural Oregon gets even more rural. Where wheat and alfalfa fields are often criss-crossed with the indelible wagon tracks of the pioneers. There the old cottonwoods and ponderosa line the rushing waters of creeks that bring mountain water down into the valley. I spread the envelope wide to see if I had missed anything that might better explain the contents.

There on the inside of the flap, probably written as an afterthought before sealing, was a single sentence. "I think I must need help."

"The game is afoot Watson," I murmured aloud, to no one in particular.

CHAPTER TWO

I made a couple of to-do list notes to myself about rescheduling the dentist, calling and confirming with my sister, cleaning my office and filing away a couple of months of paperwork. I locked up the office and headed toward the stairwell.

Hoofing downstairs is always easier.

I walked out the front building entry into the bright spring sun. I made my way through the haze created by several of the annexes various hacker population. Widespread public disfavor of tobacco addiction has recently made for some pretty loopy regulations. The whole no smoking in public buildings has expanded to the state now telling private businesses whether they can allow smoking on their own premises.

That has got to make more people than me nervous.

Whether you smoke or not, you have to raise an eyebrow when your government is marching in your front door deciding your home or business policy, then marching folks out on to the street in any kind of weather. That just doesn't speak well for the claim that we need to regulate to protect the public health.

It seems to me there are just some things you ought not try to regulate.

You would think the whole Prohibition debacle proved that bad laws just make criminals out of otherwise good people. I personally am not a tobacco user, so I used to avoid places where people smoke. Seems like a simple solution, but now the government has clustered all the smokers outside every door for my convenience.

It is like a new generation fire drill.

Ahhhh, the long arm of progress.

I wove my way through the people who no longer found smoking a way to relax and headed around the corner of the block to Goss Motors to retrieve my treasured truck.

I was able to write the check and retrieve my pick-up without visibly wincing at the expense.

I had just finished a job locating the rightful heirs to a local agricultural estate. The only daughter of the family had been the rebellious type. Deciding that the boy from a neighboring farm her parents had selected as a suitable mate was a very sorry choice, she had left home early and moved to Alaska. She had apparently thought that was enough distance to put between them.

It had been. She had completely disappeared.

Out of pre-arranged sight and mind.

The note she left was such a parental indictment they were ashamed to show it to the police. Severely chastened, mom and dad had attempted unsuccessfully to find her themselves through the years. Eventually the patriarch had passed on and the mother, seeing the inevitable end of the rainbow in her future as well, finally sought professional assistance.

It turned out to be one of those sad, serendipitous sets of circumstance. The daughter had recently, with her Alaskan backcountry, pilot husband, been the victim of a faulty fuel line accident in their twin engine. They had gone down in the mountains near their remote cabin. Their two young children had been in school at the time and had been spared. The boys had been temporarily placed in foster care since the pilot actually had no family and his wife had claimed she had none as well. They left no will. No one was aware she had a considerable inheritance to make provisions for.

The finding of their daughter had been too late, but timely for the two children who had come to the valley to be united with a grandmother of whom they had previously been unaware.

Not one to dictate family relations, I was still sort of relieved to know that the grandmother probably wasn't going to be around to try arranging any nuptials for a second generation of agricultural estate consolidation.

The delighted, elderly woman, who had, as a result, been reunited with two of her long estranged grandchildren, did bonus me more than my original bill.

As I backed out of the repair shop the mechanic was lecturing me about something that would need replacing soon.

"That alternator is eventually going to need tending, Cate," he said.

I nodded in an effort at comprehension and said I'd have it back soon.

I was feeling flush and hungry, so I indulged myself three blocks down the street with a double patty salad burger, an order of curly fries and a cherry 7-Up at Nell's N' Out, the small, gravel fronted drive-in on the east end of town.

Nell's is a throwback to the original drive in and a local landmark.

The fast food pushers out on the freeway strip had not dimmed the passion that La Grande and the surrounding residents had for Nell's. Everyone took it for granted that the food takes a little longer since it is made fresh. That had gained the small drive in the nickname Snails N' Out, but it was a term of affection and pride for a traditional drive in that has withstood the glut of fast food fads. The original identity of 'Nell' was unclear to me, but what remains is an establishment that assures longevity to forty years of Main Street cruising youth and their parents. It offers a menu that whispers, "Yes, you can go back, and you can have fries with it too!"

I love this town.

The city of La Grande has felt like my hometown from the first day I drove down into it. It did not matter that I did not arrive until I was an adult, my first trip here just felt like finally arriving home.

The summers I had spent annually with my grandparents had been in nearby Ukiah, a town about fifty miles away. I was already madly in love with the eastern half of Oregon, but I had never really been to La Grande proper until late one year at summer's end when I had pursued a Portland woman here at the request of her real estate empire-building husband.

Apparently, she had abandoned him, their three small children and their suburban ranch-style castle, in favor of following an eastern Oregon steer roper about the Northwest. She did remember to take a few important things with her, like the contents of their bank checking and savings account holdings and the surprisingly lucrative contents of their safe deposit box. That box had contained too much cash converted to expensive jewelry in my humble opinion.

That was also the opinion of her abandoned husband.

It turned out that mixed in with that pirate's trove of jewelry had been some of Mr. Real Estate's dear departed Mama's family heirlooms.

The situation had been muddied by the fact that the steer roper she had left with had no permanent address or visible means of support other than an infrequently awarded silver belt buckle.

It was obvious she liked a man who offered the potential of more jewelry.

Her deserted hubby just wanted his mother's rings and things.

He had provided no name for the cowboy; at least that was repeatable or traceable, so I ended up spending the better part of a summer following the rodeo money circuit around California, Oregon, Washington, and Idaho. He was actually difficult to track. He didn't win much and apparently only left a big impression on bored housewives.

I finally connected with the two of them in La Grande where they were laying over at some of his friends' house following the Pendleton Round Up; Oregon's uber-rodeo.

In the meantime, I had my fair share of summer rodeo boot scootin' action. I renewed my love of horse racing, developed a lasting love for cowboys, Hank Williams' music and I filled, at last count, a lifelong intake quota for corn dogs and grilled onion burgers.

Mr. Steer Roper and the former Mrs. Real Estate Empire were living the life of rodeo transients in the cramped living quarters of a combination human-horse motor home. After a couple of months of this man-beast familiarity she was almost grateful to see me arrive to serve her with papers.

The roping season appeared to be over for her.

She meekly bummed a ride home with me.

She could not wait to leave La Grande and I could not wait to get her back to Portland and return as quickly as possible to my discovery of God's Country.

I was only too happy to deliver her and what remained of Grandma's jewels to her surprisingly forgiving spouse.

He paid me very extravagantly, as real estate tycoons are capable of.

I, in turn, invested that money into a scouting trip and subsequent move back to La Grande. Another real estate transaction if you will.

I have never been sorry for that move.

I still have a soft spot for rodeos; I attend every one I physically can get to.

To this day, I still cannot force myself to eat another corn dog.

CHAPTER THREE

I drove through the afternoon bustle of Adams Avenue, La Grande's main street and turned the speaker volume up on the CD in the deck. The player was certainly 'after-market' to Sam. It held 5 discs and I had it on random select.

Today's offerings covered a range from a classical compilation, a Best of Jimmy Buffet, an old Dean Martin and a new Lyle Lovett. I had also thrown in an Etta James for sheer rumble. Music really defines moods. I seem to have lots of them. Therefore, I love lots of different varieties of music. If the truth were known, I secretly always wanted to be in a band. I do play a little guitar, but only enough to embarrass myself if someone discovers me plunking away and asks to hear me play more.

I live my dream of musicianship vicariously. I buy too many CD's at La Grande Stereo & Music and I sing way too loudly when I'm driving. I roll the windows up so as not to be arrested for creating a public nuisance. My dog has adjusted.

The first cut for this afternoon was Buffet's 'Cheeseburger in Paradise' and I was struck by how cosmically appropriate that selection was. Life really was good sitting behind the wheel of Sam my newly tuned truck with a Nell's cheeseburger in what I truly consider paradise.

There was still plenty of day left to cruise out to Union and look into the cryptic note I had discovered at the office and to see how good 'Sam' was running after his recent drain on my cash reserves. I stopped by my small house to retrieve Hoover, my Blue Heeler dog. She usually accompanies me everywhere, but had lazily chosen to sleep in this morning, a not uncommon circumstance.

My living arrangement is just right for me. It is a small house on the property of a local lawyer Bill Peterson and his wife Maggie. Their south side home had been the main residence of a once larger estate. I live in what had been the hired hand's quarters.

The multi-acre estate had dwindled as the town grew, and now occupied about a city block. My home was a secondary dwelling, often labeled a mother-in-law house, for obvious reasons. It is small, spare and has been lovingly brought back to life with renovated hardwood floors; white on white walls and the few nice antiques I have been able to acquire over the years. There are two small bedrooms, a bath, a kitchen-dining area, a screened-in back porch, which serves as a sunroom and an actual library room. The library walls are ceiling to floor built in shelves, which I have had no trouble filling from the boxes of books that I have collected, read, re-read and hauled about with me my entire life.

The house could have been a home from the 1800's, but is dated by the modern kitchen appliances and bathroom amenities. Honor thy past, but, hurray for progress.

The various inhabitants and owners throughout the years thankfully did not renovate the charming little structure out of its original exterior charm. Worn parts have been replaced, as needed, which makes it as sound as the day it was constructed.

It is an arrangement that works very well. The yard work is taken care of by the Peterson's, leaving me free to enjoy the benefits of flowers and a lush lawn, but none of the labor intensive fussing. My small house is just down a big sweeping slope from their expansive home but still affords a magnificent view of the surrounding mountains.

Although not covered in the lease agreement, it was also very handy to have the benefit of legal counsel across the lawn, and Bill has served as a sounding board often enough. His wise suggestions had several times kept me from the legal entanglements that my profession can inadvertently generate. Maggie mothers Hoover and I unmercifully.

The investigators of literature, historically, have required companionship - someone to bounce their ideas and deductions off of.

Sherlock had his 'Watson', Inspector Morse his 'Lewis', Poirot his 'Hastings' and even Miss Marple had various 'dear friends' and an errant nephew to work story problems out on. I preferred the wise-owl stare of Hoover, a five-year-old blue heeler. She creates no back talk, agrees with me completely on all theories and offers the benefit of canine protection in threatening situations.

I did not decide one day that I needed a dog. I was unaware I might want or need one. We had had a number of dogs when I was growing up, but they had generally been puppies we kids had thought were a wonderful idea. They generally grew into unruly adults and the feeding and care responsibility of my mother.

Hoover chose me, and I have been honored by her selection every day since.

About four years ago I had been spending an afternoon on the sun porch reading a lurid biographical account of Henry VIII and his marital maneuverings.

Now there was a man with serious trouble with commitment.

I glanced up to grab my iced tea off the wicker end table and there, staring in through the screen door at me, not making a move or a sound, was a mottled black and gray yearling pup with one cocked black ear. Her brown eyes met my blue ones and we instantly recognized family. I got up, opened the screen door and she trotted in, plopped down by my chair and went contentedly to sleep.

She does enjoy a good nap. I consider it like a battery charger for her energy, as she has never failed to be there for me.

Subsequent neighborhood searches and lost and found newspaper ads revealed no source from where she came. I suspected God probably thought I could use some able-bodied help. She is what you call a gift from a higher source.

Neither Hoover nor I are formally trained investigators. I have taken gun handling courses and some personal defense classes, but my formal training is completely on-the job experience. Luckily, this is a profession that benefits from street smarts over textbook reading.

I fell into this odd business after I ended up taking a job doing grunt work for a private investigator in Portland. He was a great old guy with the perfect investigator name of Lew. He was not very good at his job, but he seemed to do well enough financially. He always had more jobs than he could take on. Like many career choices, mine came with the realization that 'I could do this, and probably do it a whole lot better'.

My work resume, up until taking the job with Lew, turned out to be a patchwork of odd jobs that were a perfect training ground for investigative work.

Like most kids, I started right out of high school in the food service industry. Customer service is the basic, prime, training ground for life. You daily get the good, the bad and the ugly. Everything you ever wanted to know about human psychology can be learned waiting on others.

Those who do not have, nor ever will have servants, often become the king or queen of mean at a restaurant table. To some, the power of complaining and the need for special attention merely masks a scream of inferiority. Ultimately, you learn to pacify them. You will never win, and if the customer ain't happy, you get no gratuity and are forced to learn to live within your minimum wage. Or, worse yet, you get canned.

"Are you gonna want fries with that?" really is just an informal, investigative way of drawing more information from people. It is like saying, "Give me more details so I can better serve you. Then we both win."

I followed the minimum wage jobs by working for a few years in a camping and sporting goods store. There I received an abundant lesson in how to live without a real roof over my head and I picked up an invaluable lesson in firearms and their respective ammunition.

My dress-up-like-a-girl employment followed, which included several years in an office agency that dealt with consumer and insurance fraud. That taught me how to find the bad guys and more often than not, the good guys as well. Fascinating work, but I hated wearing nylons almost as much as the office politics.

My last relatively normal employment had been working for a horse racing stable and stall rental group out near Portland Meadows Racetrack. They had the reputation of producing a number of fairly fast ponies. From that rewarding experience I developed a lifelong love for horses of all stripes.

Especially the quick ones.

It was also where I discovered my true and future vocation.

Lew Fox, P.I., had come by the stables in the investigative employ of a local racehorse owner; a man who regularly placed out of the money and just as regularly blamed everyone except himself, or his horse.

Lew was overweight, rumpled and a chain smoker. He favored polyester pearl snap shirts and rump-sprung slacks. He looked like a used car dealer on a chop lot and he wasn't the kind of guy most people would obviously open up to and spill out all of their worldly knowledge.

He and I hit it off famously.

Up until the day he ambled into the barn where I was feeding horses, I never even considered being a private investigator as a possibility for a career move.

I was immediately smitten by the possibilities.

I followed him about for the rest of that day and several of the following ones, asking questions. In actuality, that is really what the whole job is all about. I think he found me both amusing and flattering at the same time.

Finally, after a couple of months, I wore him down to where he took me on as a kind of junior apprentice partner. He discovered I could be pretty persistent.

In investigative work, that turns out to be a real plus.

I was looking for a career direction and I was very tired of mucking stalls, feeding and exercising horses. He made room for me in his cramped office quarters in a rather unsavory area of Portland. Although he grumbled some about not having 'the time, nor inclination, to be a damn teacher' I knew he liked having the company and additional thought-process input on baffling cases.

Lew had plenty of work for us both and I turned out to be a natural born snoop. Somewhere, in the back of his mind I think he always counted on the chance that one of the eight hundred million times that he half-heartedly hit on me would prove successful. We both knew realistically there was never even the slightest possibility of that coming to fruition, but man's hope does spring eternal.

Our working relationship lasted almost four years and then the chain smoking finally tapped him on the shoulder, or rather it tapped his right lung.

Lew was not a regular-doctor-check-up kind of guy. When people used to warn him about his smoking, he would always tell them he couldn't wait to die and get to heaven. He figured that clouds were just the by-products of everyone in heaven smoking and the reward was that everyone there left you alone to smoke in peace. It was a belief that further confirmed my suspicion that everyone's view of heaven was his or her own and that there would be few disappointments for the individually righteous.

By the time his chest pains and coughing forced him in for a tune-up, his chances were pretty dismal. I stuck around for a while after he died to clean up some of his cases and to make sure his sister from California arrived to get his affairs settled. He didn't leave much that needed to be settled, but he did will me his favorite gun. It is the .38 Special I carry today.

I know in tough situations he is watching over me, and I always think of him when heavy clouds roll in.

With Lew passed on to that great smoker's paradise in the sky, the future stretched before me. I was ready for new horizons. When the opportunity presented itself for a move east, I left the city without looking back.

Although I began my investigative work in Portland, Oregon's largest metropolitan city, I never regretted moving my work to the less populated eastern side of Oregon where the jobs are fewer between, but the living is, as they say 'easy'.

CHAPTER FOUR

Hoover and I train each other regularly. She is my working partner if you will. We have developed together a communication code of hand signals and speech inflections. It incorporates some of the sibling signals I used as a child. The signals may be redundant, as I often swear she is psychic and can read my mind. She has never failed to sense when I need assistance or come to my aid. She does have a couple of flaws, one of which is that penchant for sleeping late in the mornings and the other a furtive habit of climbing up into the furniture when my back is turned.

A small price to pay for 24-hour protection.

Hoover caught the scent of burger on my breath as soon as I arrived home. She perked up her ears to see if I had indulged her as well. I produced her feast; a plain burger, on a bun, hold the condiments. She consumed hers with the same speed that I had mine and we headed out of town, south toward the community of Union.

La Grande is located in the middle of a great, round valley, which an early French Canadian fur trapper had, in a burst of inspiration, called the great round valley. Uninspired perhaps, but descriptive enough to stick.

The Grande Ronde Valley furnished the Oregon Trail pioneers of the early 1800's their first real vision of "Oregon's Promised Land". It was the first lush, green land they had seen in many weeks. The dry, sage-brushy desert to the south becomes more hospitable at the border of the Blue Mountains. The time of year that the emigrants arrived in the valley, and the scarcity of needed supplies required they press on to the Willamette Valley, but many remembered the valley's rivers and trees, its beauty and potential for abundance. Once they had reached their destination, recouped supplies and their journey weary senses, many returned to settle and enjoy the fertile land and beautiful surroundings of that great, round valley.

That same breathtaking natural wildness was all around me as I drove out old Highway 30. I rolled down Sam's windows and let the cooling spring air along Ladd Marsh ruffle my hair and Hoover's fur. Blue Heeler dogs are known for a championship ability to shed. The moving air circulated a tornado of downy, gray undercoat and then sucked it out the open window. This canine fiber factory is the primary reason I rarely wear black. I gave a chiding glance at old Hoov, but she was blissfully unaware. She dozed innocently on the seat beside me, her feet twitching in pursuit of some ethereal rabbit or stray cow.

The red-winged black birds were out in full force in the cattail choked ditches surrounding the marsh. Swooping from one cattail perch to the next, they proudly displayed their stunning red shoulder chevrons- little generals parading their sign of rank over their plain blackbird brothers.

Those birds truly know the power of accessorizing. They seem to know that a splash of red dresses up any outfit. I identify more with these birds than any other. Certainly not parrot flashy, but able to clean up nicely.

I am not particularly a beautiful woman. Heading off to Hollywood never crossed my mind when I considered career options, but I think I'm attractive in a kind of girl-next-door way.

Maybe girl-next-door-with-weapons-permit way.

I have an unruly mass of black hair and Irish blue eyes stirred into my genetic mix by my father. My after market accessory package contains a tendency to favor blue jeans and cowboy boots over business suits and heels. Pictures of me as a child are proof that I always carried a little extra weight. Good food and bad follow through on exercise have guaranteed me a roundness that prevents elderly women from worrying whether I am eating enough.

I slowed to match the speed limits as I hit the outskirts of Union. This was a small town steeped in the history of the Oregon Trail and blessed with some of the most magnificent turn of the century homes in the valley.

They also throw one hell of a rodeo and stock show in Union early each June, with a claim to fame as the oldest continuous rodeo in the Northwest. The town goes wild for a solid week and children from the surrounding counties bring the animals they have raised over the past year for judging. It is as American a summer event as any city can produce. They have horse racing each night and that is where you will annually find me, sitting in the stands each evening, hopefully clutching the proper picks.

I do not drink or smoke, but I am not absent a few vices.

I headed left out the Catherine Creek Highway and mentally blessed the fact I was able to live in these marvelous surroundings and continue to pursue my unusual female profession. Surprisingly, there were enough unclaimed heirs, missing children, errant husbands and stolen property issues to keep food and Purina on Hoover's and my table.

The houses grew less frequent the farther up the creek I traveled and as I drove I considered what to expect in what was to be an isolated country location. If someone was feeling the need to ask for help, the obvious connection was to assume there was someone or something that was causing that need. I took the small .38 revolver out of my bag and secured it into the pocket of my jacket. It was a formidable enough weapon to deter most threats and I kept myself dead center accurate with monthly practice at a gun club range out toward Ukiah.

Most of the investigative work I did involved nothing more lethal than a telephone. The bulk of the searching I did these days was by computer and the times I had actually felt myself in mortal danger were few. I had drawn my weapon in the line of work several times in the past decade, but each incident

43

had left enough of an impression to make me over-cautious and Boy Scout prepared.

I prefer mental cunning to firepower, but I am respectful of firearms. Self preservation has made me unafraid to use a gun. I have developed over time, and for that same desire for survival, an ability to compartmentalize dangerous people right along side predatory animals. Those humans who wish to do you harm deserve the same reaction as beasts in the wild that seek your quick and bloody demise.

I kept my gun in good working order, my permits active and my aim true.

CHAPTER FIVE

As I suspected, the map led me to a road that branched off the main highway, over the creek and up a very long draw lined with elderly cottonwoods, majestic ponderosas and dense brush. Clear mountain run-off had kept the gully down the draw moist and the vegetation stood out in contrast to the yellow grass hills. The snow peaks of the nearby mountain range guaranteed a heavy spring run off and more of that rich water supply.

There were fewer and fewer ranches and farms the farther out I got. It was a territory that most ranchers only use to summer over their cattle. Traffic was infrequent and mostly consisted of travel trailers headed into the mountains for recreation or pick-ups and long stock trailers hauling cow-calf pairs into the hills for the rich spring feeding opportunities.

I pulled off onto the private road and Hoover, jostled and awakened by the bouncing of the pickup over dirt ruts, was immediately alert on the seat beside me. Although I usually felt at ease with my eastern

Oregon surroundings, I was in unfamiliar, off the beaten path territory here. I felt slightly prickly around my coat collar and that apprehension transferred itself to my sensitive dog companion. She uttered a low, sustained growl and stiffened her shoulders. I reached over, scratched her ears and tried to calm us both.

"Don't you spook me too, Hoov," I squawked, realizing my throat was too dry for words.

"Get a grip," I thought to myself, "you're a hardened professional."

I laughed rather nervously and loosely rolled my shoulders just as I rounded a bend and came upon a gray, two story, weathered farmhouse. Several equally faded out buildings, all well hidden in the trees, surrounded it. I pulled up close to the front door, circling around to make sure the front of the pickup was facing back the way I had come.

"Know your entrances and exits," I said out loud.

Hoover, ears up, body rigid-tense, did not reply. She already knew this was one of our hard and fast rules.

I swung down out of the rig, and Hoover bounded out in front, a female Gallahad, motivated by curiosity as much as protection. As I approached the house, the wooden screen door opened to reveal a simply dressed woman, in her mid to late fifties, her silver-blond hair tied back to reveal a face absent of cosmetic highlight.

"You're the one Carl took the note to aren't you?" she asked tentatively, barely above a whisper. "You are the one who's come to help me?"

"I hope so," I replied, holding out my hand to shake hers. "Cate Conway, and you are?"

She grasped my hand from the top, as one would take a package that was being offered. She stepped back and motioned me in.

"Please call me Eva," she said rather formally.

I motioned Hoover down on the porch. She took up a watchful sentry, positioning herself to see me through the screen door.

The inside of the house revealed itself as spare and devoid of adornment as the outside and its inhabitant. The furniture was mostly a few straight-backed chairs, lined against grayish white walls. There was an old wood cook stove, a plain kitchen table, but no signs of a refrigerator or any modern cooking appliances.

The table held a canning jar of dried grass and early wild roses, the only visible sign of decoration. There were no pictures on the walls or curtains at the windows. It looked like a vacation getaway, or a rental cabin, inhabited only briefly from time to time; a place for second-best furniture and dishes.

Not a place where you left or kept valuables.

"Won't you sit down?" she offered nervously. "I never have company and I don't have very much to offer for refreshment. I can make us some mint tea."

"That would be very nice," I said, taking a chair at the scrubbed pine table. "Have you lived here long? I don't think I have ever been up this road and I'm sure I don't know as though I have seen you around anywhere."

She paused, midway through pouring steaming water into an old stoneware teapot.

"Well, that is part of the reason for the note, dear. I am a bit embarrassed to say, I am really not sure who I am either."

CHAPTER SIX

I tried not to look confused. She brought the pot and two cups to the table and sat down. I had obviously not known her long enough to establish any kind of sanity level, but she began a rather bizarre, unbelievable, disjointed explanation and her story did nothing to convince me that she wasn't just a confused woman who had spent maybe too long alone in the backwoods. She spoke quietly, rather formally, with no trace of colloquial slang.

Her sentences bumped into one another, as though she had been saving it all up and now it was pouring out.

"Carl, he's the young man who delivers our supplies, brought me a book of business names last week. Charles would have never allowed that sort of thing in the house, on account of needing to keep the world at arm's length, it being such a poison place, but I got so worried. Charles has never been away for this long before and I…"

I interrupted her for clarity, setting aside the 'poison place' remark for later questioning. "..and Charles would be?"

"Charles is my husband, and he has never been gone out there this long, nearly two months as near as I can figure." She paused to take a sip of her tea. "I realized if something bad has happened to him I would need to find him."

She glanced nervously about her at this moment, as if there was the potential of being overheard. Then, leaning in, she said in an even softer, defensive voice.

"That is when I found the way to unlock Charles' room. Well, I had to, you see. I am out of medicine and I thought there might be some in that room. Charles is very clear about me taking my medicine, and I get all confused and fuzzy if I don't. But, I didn't find my medicine. That is when I asked Carl to help me find someone to figure this out. He didn't know how to help. He wrote out the directions from town to here and pointed out where to look for help. It was in the book, phone listings I believe he called it, that he showed me your name."

"Phone listings, she believed he called it?" I wondered silently, "What century, or planet is she from?"

"If there is some medicine that you need a refill on, I can arrange that with your doctor," I said, thinking that a lack of 'meds' just might explain a lot about her rambling.

She began again, shaking her head, "Oh, We don't use doctors. Charles brings me my medicine. That is why I am so worried."

"You say you think Charles may be missing?" I asked. Missing persons. That was an area where I was in my element. Rambling, loony women who needed refills were an entirely different matter.

"Oh yes, I believe that must be so. He has never been gone this long before and he knows by now I would be out of medicine. He is *so* firm about me not missing my medicine every day. He makes sure I have enough each time he is gone, so I just know something is wrong."

"Tell me where he gets your medicine refilled, and *I* can pick it up for you," I offered again.

"I really don't know where Charles gets the medicine." She had her hands clasped in front of her chest, slightly wringing them.

"It is important I take my medicine," she repeated. "I am not allowed in his room, he will be so angry at me for going in, but, I was getting so confused and I just needed….. help."

I was beginning to think that this Charles fellow might be some kind of control freak, and I began hoping he wouldn't return until I had gotten a better grasp of this whole situation.

Eva went on, her hands continuing together, their quiet ballet at the front of her plain, blue cotton dress, "I wasn't prying, I was just looking for something…. something to help me find Charles and there it was in the bottom of a drawer under a lot of papers".

"What did you find Eva?" I asked calmly.

"The piece of paper about the missing girl," she said, staring straight at me, "for some reason I thought to myself, good heavens, that is about me!"

CHAPTER SEVEN

The entire situation, and my surroundings, took on a few of the characteristics of the Bates Motel. The potential of some Norman-like character rushing out of an adjoining room with a kitchen knife seemed entirely possible.

"Please don't let her offer me a nice shower," I thought.

It was obvious that this woman was confused, potentially mentally ill, and perhaps severely in need of prescription medication to stabilize her.

Her speech patterns had no regional dialect and her mannerisms were those of someone who had little practice at social interaction. It was like watching the performance of someone who hadn't learned her lines for the play well enough to go on stage.

Do you think you can find him for me?" she continued.

"First things first," I replied. "Who are you? I mean, I know you believe you may be that missing woman in the clipping, but who have you thought you were until now?"

"Eva. I know I am Eva. That is all I know, though. I can't tell you anything else, and when I try to think my head hurts and things just get all fuzzy." She stopped wringing her hands and quietly held her long slender fingers on each side of her head at her temples for a long, silent time.

She remained absolutely still. Her simple face mirrored confusion, fear and an absolute exhaustion. She was momentarily an Edward Hopper painting, bearing some title like 'Woman with Amnesia'. The lines of her body were simple and elegant and in the natural and neutral lighting she looked posed.

"I need you to think hard and tell me everything you know, so that I can help you," I ventured quietly, realizing I was committing myself to the case and realizing how appropriate the word 'commit' felt in this instance.

"I am at a loss on where to start until you help me. I can get you to a doctor…"

"Oh no!" she interrupted, the fear that had been present in the mix on her face now dominating her entire being. "I am not allowed to leave!"

My face must have looked a bit wide-eyed at her response.

"Charles only wants what's best for me. He is very protective. You live out there, you must know the dangers!" She spoke a singsong of repetition.

"Out there?" I repeated questioningly. Again I marveled at just how ill she might be.

"Yes," she explained, as if reading her lines. "Charles always goes off alone to take care of the business, so I will not be subject to all of the evil that takes place. Charles says it is wicked and it is no place for women."

Charles, wherever he might be, was going to be one interesting character. I wondered what old Charlie was going to think about a lady private-eye from "out there" sitting, taking afternoon tea with what was either a fruitcake of a wife or a terribly misinformed, captive woman.

Setting all of the wickedness of the world discussion aside for now, I realized that I was going to have to sort out exactly where to go with this situation. I backtracked to one of her earlier statements.

"You mentioned that Carl had brought me your note, who is Carl?"

"Carl brings the groceries," she said, "and he helps Charles with chores sometimes."

"Where do you think I can reach him?" I asked, hopeful that Carl might prove to be a valuable key to sorting out Eva's confused ramblings.

"Well, usually he just comes once a month with the regular supplies, and if Charles needs help he asks him then. He brought them right before Charles left and then when he came again I realized that Charles had been gone for a month. When he came again, I knew that too much time had passed and something was very wrong. That is when I asked him to help me find Charles and so he brought that book with your name in it." She smiled at me, as if the bulk of the mystery had just been solved.

"All right," I said, "How can I get in touch with Carl?"

"He will be back in another month," she said sadly, "but that is going to be too long for me not to have medicine, or to find Charles."

Her hand wringing was increasing in intensity and I reached out to place my hand over hers as a gesture of calm.

She flinched as though she had been struck.

She then dropped her hands to her sides, resting them palms up on the wooden chair seat beside her legs.

Assuming a military straightness she uttered an almost inaudible, "I am so sorry." Her eyes stretched open wide and she had the worst deer-in-the-headlights look I had ever seen.

"It's O.K.," I said, keeping my voice low and speaking slowly. "I didn't mean to startle you. I really am going to try to help you. I just need you to think hard no matter how fuzzy it seems and tell me all you can, so that I can get started. You will have to trust me. I didn't come to hurt you. I came because you sent for me and asked for my help. That is what I do best, so you and I, together, are going to find your Charles and get you some of your medicine. All right?"

For an entire minute or maybe two, she stared at me. I remained quiet sensing that this was an important moment in our connection. Then, just when I began to consider that I might have frightened her into some catatonic state, she relaxed. From the tip of her arched eyebrows and bulging eyes to her rigid shoulders she drooped and seemed to lose air like a doomed helium balloon.

"I... I don't know what to do," she whispered.

"Well, luckily I do," I said with considerable more bravado than I actually felt.

CHAPTER EIGHT

I removed the small, red leather covered notebook I kept in my jacket pocket. For the next half an hour I quietly assembled what sketchy information I could accumulate into a semblance of structure, asking periodic questions, for which she had no real answers.

In the end, what I had was not much.

She had no idea where her husband regularly went, just off to do business. The nature of that business was also unknown to her. There were no near neighbors and she went no farther than the yard or the wood storage shed out back. She calmly explained that Charles felt they were enough company for each other. Her submissive nature spoke of incredible domination and I had to keep from shivering slightly as I considered the barrenness of this house and what appeared to be an extremely isolated life.

I continued carefully probing the scattered memory of this fragile child-woman. I managed not to alarm her further, but her anxiety level was palpable. Her hands shook slightly as they were massaging each other and it did not take much to send her into an almost paralytic panic.

When I suggested we have a go at finding some more information in Charles, 'room' I thought she would faint dead away.

"No!" she all but shrieked, "that would not be allowed."

It took every persuasive power I had to convince her that without exploration, we were at a dead end and finding her husband would probably hinge on some piece of paper or scrap of information. You could read the fear and indecision on her face, but in the end she reluctantly showed me the room. It was down a narrow hall and although the chipped beige door was closed tight, there were signs that a lock hasp had been pried from the door.

"Carl helped me with that," she said, almost too quiet for me to hear. Her eyes fixed in slight horror where the wood had been gouged like a fresh wound. She would not enter the room, but stood clutching at the door jam as I stepped inside.

I almost stepped back in reflex. In contrast to the plainness of the rest of the home, this was like a carnival midway. Bright colors swirled on the walls and floor. There was a slight pungency to the room that I finally recognized as a spice, like clove. I realized, as my eyes focused in the dimming late afternoon light, that the riotous mass of color came from vintage 1960's music posters. They covered the walls, almost top to bottom. The clove-y smell, in that context, registered as incense of some sort.

Whatever preconceived impression I had of good old Master of the Castle Charles, this was one humdinger of a surprise. The room was a testament to flower power, a psychedelic shrine that seemed as incongruous in this setting as a peacock in a hen house.

I turned to look at Eva and saw that her eyes were cast down in that submissive posture.

"These are Charles' things, you must not touch them. He has saved them for many years. They are worth a lot… to him." Her words were the echo of a memorized command.

I gazed around me at what probably were some fairly valuable artifacts of life on the Pacific Coast during the heyday of psychedelics and the counter culture era. Twisted, balloon-fat letters proclaiming dates and times and chronicling names of musical groups and venues that had, for the most part, faded away into the ether of history like the cannabis smoke that had fueled their existence. Nestled amidst this riot of colorful graphics were some genuine collector prints; the recognizable advertising of the Grateful Dead at Winterland, the Jefferson Airplane at Portland's Crystal Ballroom, the Doors at an outdoor festival in Seattle. There were rock artist renderings here that I had seen priced in at least five figure categories. Charles had quite a collection going and I wondered with their potential worth, why he had not thought to preserve their fragility behind framed glass.

"I am not going to disturb things Eva, we talked about this. Please relax. Maybe you should go sit down at the table and I will be right there as soon as I check a few things."

She made a move as if to go, and then just eased to the floor. She did not let go of the doorjamb, so her fingers made a high pitched squealing noise as she sank. After surreptitiously checking to see that she still remained conscious, I continued my scan of the room. I realized early into my visit that the house probably ran without power. Kerosene, oil lamps and candles were everywhere in abundance and the lack of a refrigerator in the kitchen spoke volumes about the rustic nature of her existence. The early evening fading of light and Eva's hypersensitivity to my presence in this forbidden space meant I would need to move fast.

I moved across the room to a large oak bureau and picked up a small color photo in a thin wooden frame from the dresser top. It was a somewhat younger Eva and a tall broad man with sharp features and a rooster crest of black hair.

"Is this Charles?" I asked, glancing back at her. She nodded and bowed her head again. Unwilling at the moment to go through the argument of my needing to identify him versus leaving everything as I found it, I quietly slipped it into my jacket pocket. I turned my attention back to the wooden dresser and opened the top drawer.

Eva's obviously fearful compliance meant that the one door latch had been deemed sufficient to block intrusion. Nothing in the room needed further forcing. The drawers, one after the other, were lined with men's clothing, all folded with military precision, stacked and arranged in neat piles. Wildly colored t-shirts and

Henley's and tidily arranged blue jeans. Underneath the clothing, each of the drawers contained a filing system of paperwork, photos and receipts. There were divisions for Union, and Portland. Each section had folders, alphabetized and labeled in a crisp black print. In keeping with the neatness of the clothing system there were no bent folder edges, no filed papers peeking out the tops or sides. Neat, control freak that he probably was, I momentarily thought that I could use a touch of old Charlie's obsessiveness in my bulging, under-filed system back in my office.

That fleeting thought was quickly replaced with the realization that a little of Charles was probably way too much.

In the Union file there was a section, which contained hardware and grocery receipts, and surprisingly, tucked in the bottom of a file of past Union County tax receipts were some odd receipts from Cascade Locks, a small town in the Columbia Gorge. Given the almost military precise neatness of the rest of the filing system, those receipts were oddly out of place. Each of the bundled stacks was in progressive date order. No surprise there. The groceries had come from a market in Union and one called the

Alder Street Grocery in La Grande. That would at least get me to the grocery deliveryman Carl, which might provide me with some rational explanations. I saw no pharmacy receipts and no indication of what medicines I should be picking up for Eva. Equally absent were pay stubs for Charles or any calendar or planner schedule for where he might be.

Overlord and master that he might be, there was the possibility that he *could* be somewhere in need of assistance and that was another wish of Eva's; find her missing Charles.

"*Ummmmm,*" I thought, "*a little rigid aren't we Charlie old boy?*"

"That is not where I found the paper," the words came softly from the pile that was Eva in the doorway. "It was in that other dresser, over there by the window." She continued to watch my every move like a wounded hawk, protective and fearful at the same time.

I crossed to the matching bureau and pulled open the top drawer. No socks, shirts or sharp creased pants here, nor were there neat filing folders beneath. It appeared to be blankets and stored linens. If Charles had hid the clipping here, it was not meant to be found.

I had just turned to head back toward the other bureau to further explore why Charles had double hidden the Cascade Locks file when I heard a gasp from behind me. I turned and saw that Eva's head had snapped back, widening her eyes and causing the pale blue veins of her neck to protrude slightly.

"It's Charles," she hissed, "I just heard Charles! He's here!" Her voice was a startled mixture of relief, excitement and pure unadulterated fear. "I think he may be coming up the driveway!"

Hoover's low, rumbling growl and her pad of paw prints across the front porch seemed to accompany Eva's startled shout like a soundtrack.

Adrenaline hammered me in the chest and legs like I had run a four-minute mile. My body worked in a frenzy to scramble and replace folders and shut drawers. While my hands busied themselves like a five-year-old caught in the candy, my mind calmly 'noted to self' that anyone as detail attentive as Charles would know from the mangled door jam that his inner sanctum had already been breached by some pretty snoopy company.

Eva was scrambling to her feet, smoothing her hair and clothing. She started toward the kitchen and I called her to a stop.

"Eva, wait! What say we close up here first?"

She turned, her mouth slack, arms down at her sides, and then started down the hall like she hadn't even heard me.

I glanced about, realizing that any further clean up efforts were useless and started down the hall after her.

CHAPTER NINE

By the time I reached the kitchen, she stood in the door; the screen swung wide, her shoulders hunched in confusion, staring down the road at nothing. Hoover, alerted by her focus, bristled and faced the same direction.

"It was just my dog, Eva," I said quietly, "Why don't you come back in now." This had been a stressful day for her and I should never have let her manic jumpiness affect me like it had.

She allowed me to escort her back into the kitchen area but became wild-eyed and panicky when I attempted to head back to Charles' room to continue my search. I sat back at the table with her, calmed her down and promised her that I wasn't going to do anything to upset her. She kept saying that all she wanted was to lie down and rest. We were getting nowhere, so I decided to let her do just that and start fresh in the morning.

I began preparations to leave. Still shaking off the muscle tenseness brought on by wild panic, I assured her that I would return in the morning. I explained that I would try to find Carl and we could start with a better handle on things tomorrow. Carl might even be able to help with the medication question.

I tried for about twenty minutes to talk her into accompanying me, explaining I was capable of protecting her, but knowing her fear of 'out there', I was not surprised by her adamant refusal. Her saucer-sized eyes betrayed such a fear of making a trip out into the big, bad world I gave up before I lost whatever level of comfort and camaraderie we had spent the afternoon establishing. I hoped by some measure that the confidence I could gain by a prompt return in the morning might convince her to try a brief trip to town for a needed medical review.

I settled her with a fresh cup of tea, offered to make her something to eat, which she smiled and refused. I loaded Hoover and myself into Sam the truck and cheerily waved my way off down the driveway. As I bounced down the long access road I thought how it seemed like I had been there much longer than a couple of hours.

We hadn't talked about my fees but that was only part of what we still had to cover.

I reached the main highway and tried not to welcome or feel such a guilty, overwhelming, grateful relief and such a sense of normalcy returning. It felt like driving out of some spiritual dark into the light. My reeling brain cells were working to compartmentalize the patchwork of information Mary had provided. I was trying to sort the plausible from the fearful and my concentration was off just enough to make me careless.

The sun was in the process of turning the western horizon a fuchsia-gold. A sliver of the sun's remains on the hilltop flashed my eye and caused a blind spot. I pulled out onto the main road directly into the path of a big Chevy pick-up pulling a matching, gunmetal-gray horse trailer. The rig swung wide, tires whining, and slowed to a stop. Just as I was working on bringing my heart rate back to a normal target range and opening my door to go offer humble apologies to the irate pickup truck driver, the truck pulled out spitting gravel and headed on up the Catherine Creek highway.

I breathed a sigh of relief. The driver was obviously perturbed at me, but unhurt. I felt like an idiot. I had just gotten Sam back from the shop and I didn't need to crunch in his fender now that his insides were humming. I settled back onto Sam's safe, wide front bench seat, buckled up and headed back toward town, still trying to shake both the near accident and the surreal events of the last couple hours.

Hindsight is cheap, but it can be spent countless ways, buying many different conclusions. I did not know, however, at that moment, if I could have changed things, or what a very different situation I would find when I returned the next day.

CHAPTER TEN

The drive back through the city of Union to La Grande gave me about a half-hour of plan time. I have a couple of favorite times of day, very early morning and just before dark. Things seem to be in flux, either just starting or just ending. To me it is a mood elevator. I do my best thinking then, although currently I did not have much information to piece together.

The Union grocery stores were buttoning up for the night. The Alder Street Grocery would be closed by the time I returned, so tracing 'supply delivery Carl' would have to wait till morning. My only other avenues to pursue were the news clipping about the missing girl and the small, framed picture of Charles and Eva in my jacket pocket. I pulled it out and held the photo up in front of the steering wheel as I drove.

The picture wasn't recent. It could easily be as old as ten or twelve years. Eva's long hair was still clasped back, but there were fewer gray strands. Her eyes in the picture looked heavy-lidded, showing that same world-weariness that drooped her shoulders and sagged at the corners of her mouth. She wore a plain-bird, cotton shift and no jewelry or make-up.

Charles, on the other hand, more than made up for the dullness of his mate. His thick black hair was swept back and hung slightly to his shoulders. Under a dark black jacket he wore what looked like a multi-color tie-dyed collarless shirt. Around his neck a chain held a hammered, silver medallion. I couldn't make out exactly what the necklace fob was without taking my eyes off the road too long, but it looked like planet earth. It certainly was an adornment that matched his poster collection. I focused my attention on his face.

Strong, angular cheekbones dominated his features. He stared directly into the camera without smiling. His was not a 'say cheese' kind of face. Where Eva's look was soft and slack, his was hard, almost rigid. His arm around her shoulders did not pull her in with affection, but seemed to grip her steady, like one would hold and pose with a cardboard cutout.

I wondered at who had snapped the picture and where it had been taken. Who had gotten close enough to this odd couple to capture them in celluloid? The background was green bushes and blue sky that revealed nothing. Was it at their home or 'out there' in Charles' self defined, wicked world?

I got to La Grande knowing the newspaper offices were closed for the day. I drove by to find I had just missed library hours. Both places were valuable reference sources and had decades of archived newspaper records on file that might solve at least the clipping portion of the problem.

Research would have to wait until the morning as well.

My next stop was the local cop shop. The station was a combination that housed both the La Grande City Police and the Union County Sheriff. I left a message for the sheriff, sketchily explaining a potential cold case and asking that he call as soon as he arrived in the morning. I wanted to verify that Eva's suspicions of her being the missing person had some merit, and I feared sending a deputy to knock on her door in the middle of the night.

Charles had created in her a paranoid fear of the outside world and authorities in general. That, in and of itself, was fairly suspicious. Did Charles have cause to avoid legal entanglements? I was thankful, for the moment that Charles was at least temporarily missing in action. Two months gone was enough to alarm any spouse, even one as overwhelmed and skittish as Eva.

His absence just might turn out to be more of a blessing than the problem that Eva seemed to currently think it was. Despite my increasing wariness of Charles' character, Eva seemed to be utterly devoted to him. Go figure.

My mother had often given me the lovely little talk about how "there was someone out there for everyone, if one only bothered to look." That conversation had inevitably ended with her less than subtle inquiry concerning "didn't I think it was time I bothered looking?"

Given Mom's poor track record on finding the perfect mate, I usually took her suggestions with more than one grain of salt. It was inevitably, at times like this when I considered this miserable relationship I was being asked to reunite, that I thanked my bloody, lucky stars how cautious I was about entanglements.

In fact, I was currently 'in between' suitors.

My last relationship had ended when the gentleman in question took a job in a large city out of state. It was, for him, a good career move. I was unwilling to relocate and we had known for some time that our connection was fraying. It ended well and we continue to communicate.

Know your entrances and exits.

There were a couple of nice 'guy friends' who filled my dance card periodically. I am in no hurry to complicate any boy-girl matters.

Hoover waited for me in the pick-up with an air of noble patience. Knowing that I was safe in the police station, we both knew she spent every moment I had been away from the truck sound asleep. I ruffled the top of her head, promised her dinner and drove us home. I was eager for a good night's sleep in preparation for what I suspected might prove a long day tomorrow.

I was not successful with the getting a good rest portion of my plan. I slept badly, tossing and turning all night. My dreams were filled with rock music and pulsating, light show globs of color. Through the throbbing scene wandered flower children, their faces blank and devoid of emotion.

I was correct about the next day being *very* long.

CHAPTER ELEVEN

I was up, as usual, before the sun had completely made its entrance over the eastern rim of the valley. It was going to be a cloudless day and when I let Hoover out for her morning yard inspection, I caught the heady, thick smell of lilacs in the morning breeze. The large bush at the corner of the house was in full, deep purple bloom. For a moment I stopped, breathing in spring and envying the simplicity of bees. No responsibilities beyond striking a little flying insect fear into the occasional human, regular pollination of your choice of flower and, as a result, producing a product like honey.

Ahhh, the bee's life. No weird, abusive husbands, no psychotic wives or unsolved history mysteries. Just hummin' along, singin' a song.

I had just finished plunging down the handle of the coffee press pot when my phone rang. Sheriff Dan Mickey seemed unnaturally bright and cheerful to someone who had had so little sleep as I. A poor soul such as I who had not yet received the morning affirming benefits of caffeine.

"What time do you get to work, anyway?' I pretended to grumble, a habit, because that is how we interact.

"Many of us don't have the benefit of setting our own bankers hours and we actually have to do real work for a living, " he countered.

Dan Mickey had been elected sheriff of Union County for more terms than people could count. It was because they didn't think to count. He was so natural in the position that people just assumed and took it for granted that he was and always would be top man in the Sheriff's office. For a fellow late into his fifties, he was in amazing physical shape. He ran, lifted weights and managed to keep up with a cadre of deputies half his age. Children flocked around him and he knew all of their names and the names of their brothers and sisters before them. He was good natured and jovial with adults and seemed more a family member than an enforcement official. He had a confidence and strength that had watered countless flammable situations.

Tales of Dan Mickey are legend in this region. It embarrasses him to hear them. You have to consider the measure of truly remarkable people are those who are comfortable in their own skin and quiet in their greatness. It is usually the not so worthy that need constant edification or praise, or that are repeatedly reminding you of their worth.

Dan Mickey would be the last person on earth to tell you about the time he had stopped a car weaving down the I-84 freeway and had discovered in it a father and mother too drunk to get their two small children home safely. In the highly charged stress of Dan's efforts at subduing the enraged father, coupled with the mother screaming drunken, vulgar obscenities, one of the children, a tiny girl of four: unhindered by any form of car seat restraint, leapt fearfully from the back seat into oncoming traffic.

Dan did not hesitate. He dashed after her.

She suffered only the minor scrapes of being thrown clear.

One skull fracture, four leg surgeries and a legal adoption procedure later, Dan was able to be present at that child's high school graduation.

There had been no formal church service that had made him Heidi's unofficial godfather; it had been his own personal assignment. Dan's wife Elaine told me once that he had kept a hawk's vigil on that small family unit, and true to form, his and theirs, he had been there three years later when the birth mother and father had finally lost their parental rights. Heidi and her younger brother Justus had come to be swallowed up, at first informally and finally legally, into the Mickey clan.

Dan would not tell tales like that about himself and that is what makes him more precious and the stories more meaningful to all his many friends and extended family.

The Mickeys were a large, boisterous family that had its share of joy and pain but they always seemed to have another place at the table or could find the precious time to attend one more school recital, baseball or soccer game.

They have always treated me like family and I have watched in awe and a little sadness at the simple abundance that a normal, loving, mom and dad home life could provide. It did not insulate them from problem children or life's serrated edges, but it did provide a priceless foundation.

I had known Dan for the better part of two decades. He had made me and my work efforts welcome from the very first day we met. I counted on his advice and his friendship. He was a lot like, and reminded me of, my older brother, who had once been a state trooper in Washington.

Dan Mickey had tried, on countless occasions, to encourage me to pursue a formal career in law enforcement, but I am more comfortable with the freedom of setting my own hours and I truly hate taking orders.

"Too much independence in my nature," I would tell him. "It's a character flaw, and besides tan uniforms bring out the sallow in my complexion."

He was his usual teasing self early this morning.

"What kind of mischief are you up to that would warrant a visit to the station last night?" he asked. "Some kind of trouble you need me to drag you out of?"

I always made a point to let local law enforcement know what was going on during the course of my investigations. It saved complicated explanations down the road. Several times it had proved beneficial, with my being blessed with some severely needed back up.

I gave him a brief run-down of the skeletal information I had accumulated. He was unfamiliar with the reclusive residents up Catherine Creek, but did remember the Milton girl's disappearance.

"I was a 'fresh out of the academy' deputy back then and I remember we spent a good bit of time looking for her. She was a very pretty girl as I recall."

"Well," I said, "this may or may not have anything to do with anything. She isn't even sure she is 'her". I am going to go dig in a bit at the library, and I'll call you later if it looks like anything. Just in case though, you might think about dusting off those old files.

"Hell hath no fury like an ancient filing system", he groused.

CHAPTER TWELVE

Hoover snored softly in the over-stuffed chair I had given up trying to keep her out of. I put down fresh kibble and replenished her water. I grabbed an apple and a chunk of cheddar for my own breakfast and headed off to the La Grande Public Library. I entered the old Carnegie brick building and breathed in the combination scent of shelved books and wood polish. It was a normal, everyday comfort smell that some might take for granted. To me it was an aroma as comforting as warm bread.

It took me to first days of grade school and high school study halls. Libraries are the original safe homes on the block and they have sheltered me often when I was out of sorts or seeking quiet, familiar ground.

When I was growing up in the most rural parts of Oregon, the Bookmobile would show up on Saturdays. It would wheeze to a stop in the large parking lots of the various state fish hatcheries where my father was gainfully employed and spent his off-hours drinking like the fish that he tended. It was a large, lumbering, sea green vehicle whose accordion doors would open up like the doors to a travel agency and the inside would reveal stories about everything in the world. I would easily secure the book limit I was allowed to check out and devour them long before it was time for the mobile library's return.

Books often prove to be a distraction and escape from troubled times or homes. Mine was certainly that. As an adult, I still feel a sense of 'I get to go on a journey' excitement whenever I wander the aisles of a library or bookstore deciding what will leap off the shelf to capture me.

I got there just as it opened and at this early hour Joan, the librarian, and I were alone in the building.

I did a little mental calculation of Eva's approximate age, and asked her for a span of about ten years worth of old newspaper files. I set myself up at the microfiche machine in the back corner and smiled as she brought a box back to where I was sitting. I could have cajoled much of this information out of Dan Mickey's police files, but that was an avenue and an effort that might not prove to be necessary. He did not need to furnish me information at all, and often couldn't, so I was appreciative when he could and respectful enough to dig up my own information and earn my own salt.

"Are you working on a big case, Cate?" Joan asked in a voice that was curious but casual in an effort not to pry.

My line of work is a novelty at best in this town and the fact that I am fairly short, a female and look more like a store clerk than Sam Spade is a constant source of wonder to the people I live amongst.

"It's just lucky for me the world will never run out of bad guys or lost cats," I teased.

She smiled back and returned to restocking the shelves.

The search did not take long. I had the May 12th date on the clipping as a solid reference and as luck would have it, that specific day rolls around only once annually. I located the identical news article I had received taped to my office door, as well as several others that had run in the weeks before and after.

It had all happened several years before had I moved to La Grande, and although the story was new to me, it was an all too familiar one, given the era when it occurred and its similarity to other stories that had played out across America. It was a time when the nation's youth were turning on, tuning in and dropping off the face of the planet; or at least out of the grasp of their parental confines.

The disappearance of a local girl was naturally newsworthy, but this story had warranted extra ink. It provided all the bells and whistles that fueled dinner table conversation. This was more than just a girl gone missing. It whispered the tawdry lure of sex, drugs and rock and roll.

Apparently Mary Milton had not been a resident of La Grande for very long. Her father, a general practice physician, had been drafted by the growing local hospital to join the staff some four years earlier. Mary, an only child, had been away attending college back east when her father had transferred his practice. Her arrival, quietly brought home by her parents, had been relatively unknown until her reported disappearance. Her father, desperate to locate her, had been forthcoming with information, both to the police and the newspaper reporter.

Several months before Mary's disappearance, Dr. Milton had reportedly engaged the assistance of a private investigator. Unanswered phone calls and letters had alarmed he and his wife enough to attempt to locate his daughter. It turned out she was not back east, finishing an extremely expensive education in the ivy covered halls of Vassar, her mother's alma mater, but was instead living a rather lurid existence at a large hippie commune in the California hills.

A report to the local police had been the probable cause California officials had been waiting for. A rescue-raid on the flower children's compound had successfully reunited a reluctant Mary with her frantic parents. It had also turned up enough illegal substances and parole violators to disband the loud, colorful circus of a civic problem that the commune had become.

Communal living was not a new phenomenon, but the 1960's brought the concept into the forefront and threw it onto the doormat of the Leave it to Beaver 1950's. The very concept was, by its title, a bad match to follow the communism paranoid times of the Joe McCarthy era.

The Free Love generation gave the 'all for one and one for all community' wings, or horns in some cases.

Like many of the hippie or Marxist concepts, the utopian idea of everyone sharing equally from the same pot usually ended badly. People may be strange, but they are not carbon copies. Anyone who has ever had to share a bedroom with a sibling or tried moving into a dorm room with total strangers can relate to how quickly petty differences can become the cannon fodder of civil wars. Mix in a little mind or mood altering chemistry experimentation, illegal activity, paranoia and some genuine personality disorders and most communal visions got blurry in a hurry.

After returning home to La Grande with their stumbling, nearly unrecognizable daughter, the Milton's had spent considerable expense working with an agency that specialized in the de-programming of susceptible flower children. They spent an equal amount of time working their daughter through the withdrawal stages of a dependence on several recreational drugs; pharmaceuticals that Dr. Milton had rare opportunity to prescribe or be familiar with in his everyday practice.

The recovery process of their daughter had been difficult but eventually successful. Throughout the ordeal Mary had revealed little regarding the details of her transcontinental relocation other than she had apparently been swept up and westward by a boy she had met at a campus folk concert. Knowing that her change of career focus and address would most certainly alarm her parents, she had opted to just not tell them.

Vassar, like all institutes of higher learning at the time, was experiencing the confusing tornado of sit-ins, equal rights and war resistance. The siren call of a new generation drew many American youth from the confines of their homes, schools and occupations to the West Coast. That was where 'It' was happening.

Mary had been one of the lemmings in that migration.

Like many parents caught up in the upheaval of that decade of peace and love and who experienced the alienation of their once docile offspring, Dr. and Mrs. Milton were unprepared for and shocked by the transformation of their daughter and by her chosen living conditions.

Mary had apparently been 'cozied up' with ten or twelve other young people in a teepee in Marin County. The back to native housing shelter had been one of several similar structures set up on a piece of rural property that one of the commune's members had recently inherited.

According to Mary's father, sanitation had been marginal, as there were no facilities capable of handling the drainage needs of nearly one hundred pot smoking, psychedelics and beer consuming young adults who were indeed living the 'high' life.

Bingo. California zoning violation number one.

The property was rural enough to keep neighbors from regularly complaining about the astounding and constant music decibels, but traffic to and from the encampment was steady and increasingly dangerous to the neighbors and their livestock.

Dr. Milton had been proud to report their raid had effectively scattered the commune and its inhabitants and sent multiple children back to the homes they came from.

'Good riddance' had been his words.

I thought that it might have been a bit naïve to think that an out-of sight-out-of-mind dispersal was probably less than a permanent solution to the problem of runaway children and the drug high life, but who knew?

The fact that their daughter had been physically separated from that influence had worked to the

Milton's advantage. Reportedly, the once healthy color returned to her hair and skin. Although they felt the experience had undoubtedly left her some internal physical and emotional scarring, externally all that remained was a tiny shoulder tattoo, a small depiction of earth with two parallel lines through its center. It had been a sign of the commune, a group logo or marking, a brand to show commitment to each other. Mary had refused to talk about it or remove it and her parents had let it go.

Sadly, it was a mark the Milton's hoped would help identify their daughter if she were found.

I pulled the picture of Charles and Eva from my jacket pocket. It was grainy, but I was almost sure Charles' necklace was that same image.

Mary had, to her parent's relief, been showing signs of her old self. She was and always had been a beautiful girl with promise. She seemed to be picking up the pieces of her life, and had just begun taking a few art and theatre classes at what was referred to then as Eastern Oregon College when, without a word or note, she vanished on an afternoon walk to the market.

"We were baking together and didn't have all of the ingredients for chocolate chip cookies," her tearful mother had reported. "She was just going to pick up what we needed." It had been a typical mother-daughter activity that had seemed refreshing and so rewarding after the many months of struggle and abnormality.

None of Mary's belongings were missing. There was no indication she had made plans to pack up and return to the California hills from where she had been located. A subsequent call to authorities had verified that the merry band of flower children had indeed moved on to more hospitable surroundings without a forwarding address. Mary had not boarded the Amtrak train nor had she been a Greyhound bus passenger.

She had not been in town long enough to have made many friends that might provide information, male or female. Other than a few students who had attended classes with her, she had not connected with many young friends who even knew she was a resident. There had been no reports of suspicious vehicles in the area, nor reports of a slim girl with waist length blonde hair, entering or being forced into one.

The Milton's had provided a photo of their one and only child. You could tell it had been her high school graduation picture. They hoped the picture would spark someone in the community's memory or recognition. Apparently the effort had been unsuccessful, as nothing had turned up and no one, outside a small group of family friends and a couple of professors, had even recognized her.

But I did.

CHAPTER THIRTEEN

Eva, or as it turns out, Mary, had been a beautiful young woman. A wide, confident smile revealed the even teeth that spoke of pre-teen braces. She had chosen a fuzzy scoop neck sweater and small diamond necklace for her senior moment. A tiny, sparkling butterfly clip held her slightly teased hair parted off to one side. Her's was not the wild-eyed, flower power look that was beginning to pervade the high school crowds of that time. This was a girl who would have her sights set on the pursuit of teaching, or one of the new employment opportunities finally opening up for assertive young ladies. The news clippings had not revealed where she had attended high school, but I would have bet real money that her photo in her high school annual would be accompanied by a lengthy list of achievements, participation in business clubs, sporting activities, drama and probably student leadership.

There was very little left of this girl in the fragile woman who had summoned me to what was more a rural prison than a home. How in the world could she be living about twenty miles from where she was abducted, and have no recollection of any of this? Had she been this close all this time? If she had been abducted, wouldn't that person, or persons, have wanted to take her where they wouldn't run the risk of her escaping or being recognized? If it hadn't been foul play, and she had been wandering aimlessly with some sort of post drug dependant amnesia, wouldn't someone have found her and sought medical attention for her?

This had been a young, college-educated woman. What had reduced her to the 'Stepford Wife' ghost that I had spent the day with? Who would have taken her and broken her spirit so completely? She was a married woman for heaven's sake. Why would anyone marry someone who didn't know who she was or where she had come from?

Would the answer to any or all of these questions turn out to be Charles? If it had been he who had taken her, it might explain why she was discouraged from wandering out into the big, evil world.

I made copies of the Mary articles and paid for them at the counter. Librarian Joan recommended a new autobiography that had just come in and was available and I sadly declined, knowing that my opportunity to relax with a good book was going to be severely compromised until I had the whole Eva-Mary situation sorted out.

I called Sheriff Mickey from my cell phone in the car and suggested either he or an available deputy might want to accompany me out to Eva's place. She was in for quite a shock. Who knew what kind of reaction a uniformed officer would generate? Hopefully the time we had spent together had connected us and she could trust me enough to allow me to bring her back to town. I waited in front of the library until I saw the Sheriff's tan car pull in behind me.

I hopped in beside him and we swung by my house to pick up the now eager to go Hoover, before we started out toward Union. Hoover hopped into the caged back seat, a familiar position. She had proudly done ride alongs with the sheriff on many occasions and was in her element with the sirens and activity involved with that police work. She was unaware that she possessed none of the formal police dog training of Jingo, the sheriff's office German Shepherd, but Hoover had a street fighter kind of instinct and a natural, innate sense of which humans to trust and which to watch. She adored Sheriff Mickey and he had grown to appreciate her natural abilities and her protective, intelligent nature.

Dan Mickey apparently had taken some time to find and review the old files, because he added a bit more to my growing cache of information.

"People just kinda assumed that, given the fact she had such a fresh history of disappearing, she had just gone back and reconnected with that Mother's Helpers freak group."

"Mother's Helper's" I asked. "Was that the commune's name?"

"Yeah, supposed to be a play on them all working to save Mother Earth and a kind of tongue-in-cheek drug reference all rolled into one."

"Rolling Stones song," I remarked absently, "about Valium as I recall."

"Even straight, young police cadets knew that." he said wryly, and then added, "Turns out the Helpers were a pretty nasty bunch, more drugs and free love than peace and harmony. We didn't have much luck tracing them. They holed up down in the Haight

District for a while and that was like trying to find Bozo at a clown convention. It ended up we ran out of resources to follow the case too long. We eventually turned it over to the California authorities."

"What happened to her folks?" I asked, " I couldn't find a Dr. Milton in the phone book, working or retired."

They ended up transferring out of town; moved back east when it became evident the girl wasn't going to turn back up around here. For awhile they would call to check for news, but eventually they just didn't call back here anymore."

"*So close and yet too far*," I thought.

I felt a bit like I was riding to the rescue. A couple of decades late perhaps, but we were going to finally bring a lost, young girl home.

By the time we reached the drive into Eva and Charles' place, I had almost convinced the sheriff that Eva's shaky paranoia would require kid gloves. We were going to have to be very gentle breaking all this information to her.

"If what she is saying about needing constant medication is true, who knows what that could be, or what affect not taking it might have," I had explained.

"Given the girl's past drug complications, that could be just about anything," Dan had replied, with a touch of sarcasm that I knew came from seeing too many people waste too many years in the destructive pursuit of altered consciousness.

"She doesn't seem like an addict," I said. "She seems to fear angering Charles by missing her medicine more than struggling to maintain a high."

"Addiction can make folks pretty devious, Cate." He was staring straight ahead, one broad hand resting flat on the top of the steering wheel. I knew, without his speaking another word, he was thinking about Christopher.

Christopher Mickey was the youngest son of the Sheriff and his wife Elaine. Chris was a star athlete; the class valedictorian and running back on the football team with a guaranteed full ride scholarship to a small mid-western university. The golden boy, who had it all, lost it when he was introduced to uppers, tiny white cross-top speed pills, late in his senior year.

"Some folks seem to take to the stuff more than others," Dan had sadly told me once. His voice had been full of pain and frustration, as he had pondered the sad tale of his much loved son.

"Chris said he was only going to take some to help him study for his finals and the SAT's, then he just up and fell of the cliff. Pretty soon the pills weren't enough and he was head long into anything he could get his hands on. Mostly meth, we just can't seem to keep that crap out of the county."

Methamphetamine. Crank. Speed. An insidious drug that is as life destructive as it is addictive. The relative ease with which it can be concocted in clandestine home labs, creates an almost endless supply of it. That supply, with a little help from entrepreneurial home chemists had insinuated its way into the lives of increasing numbers of middle and high school age kids.

The sheriff's cruiser was silent except for the occasional squawk from the dispatch radio. Dan and I wound our way along the two-lane toward Catherine Creek, each lost in our own thoughts. His face was unreadable, but I guessed he was thinking about the wasted life of a son he rarely saw. A son that, even being a parent in a strong family unit and as well educated in the drug culture as a county sheriff was, he could not stop or help.

I was thinking that I hadn't known Chris Mickey as well as his brothers and sisters, but I had mourned with the rest of the community his repeated arrests and failed court imposed re-hab efforts. I know the helpless heartbreak it caused Dan and Elaine and what it must have done to the Milton's as well. There was an irony in the present situation. We were on our way to rescue a woman, once a young promising student, who, like Chris Mickey, gave it all up to get high.

Thirty odd years later and we were still fighting drug addiction and the impact that it has on our day-to-day society.

Exploring your subconscious. Better living through chemicals. It had all seemed like such a '60's flower-power lark.

"Groovy, man," I unconsciously said aloud.

Dan glanced at me, turned his eyes back to the road and just snorted in agreement.

CHAPTER FOURTEEN

Dan reluctantly agreed I would make the initial contact with Eva. If the news we came to deliver wasn't mind warping enough, having a uniformed officer at the door could easily put her over the edge. I wasn't sure how much of a mind our Eva-Mary had left to warp. We also both concurred, given her youthful history of counterculture activities, there was a good chance she would not view Sheriff Dan Mickey as a knight in shining cruiser come to her rescue.

I told Dan to let Hoover and I out half way up the winding lane to her home. He shut the engine off and promised to wait a bit for me to calm the situation. It had taken a great deal of discussion to get that grudging concession. He was still pleading his case as we got out of the cruiser.

"What if this guy Charles is back up there now, Cate? If he is part of her disappearance he might go nuts. We don't know how squirrelly this guy is."

Oh, I had a pretty good idea how squirrelly he was, but aloud I said, "She expects me back and if he is there, I will just make my excuses and come back for you. If anything gets weird, I have Hoover. Believe me, you will hear her bark from down here."

He was still shaking his head doubtfully as I headed off up the road.

Hoover padded up a couple of feet in front of me and I called her back to heel. My tone caused her caution sensors to go off and she picked up her ears and bristled her neck hairs. The short hairs at the back of my neck were prickly as well. I took a deep breath of the warm morning air and that calmed me immensely. I reached my hand into my jacket pocket and felt the cool metal of the Airweight Smith & Wesson .38.

That calmed me even more.

I rounded the last bend in the lane and positioned my travel path nearer to the pine trees that flanked the roadside. Everything was quiet except for a couple of birds that seemed to be wrapped up in the joyful moment of spring. The place looked much as I had left it the evening before. There was no vehicle announcing our sailor Charlie home from the sea, but I took no chances. I moved from tree to tree until I was near the gray, weather worn porch.

Keeping half of a massive old Ponderosa between the door and me, I called out, "Eva? Are you there? Eva? It's me Cate." I raised my voice a notch and called again, "Eva, can you hear me?"

There was no sound. I drew my gun and held it barrel up in my right hand, the butt-end cupped with my left.

Hoover, at my side until I began calling out, sensed it was time to move out. She was immediately on the porch sniffing around the door. It was a head down canvas of the ground that she usually reserved for other dogs, neighborhood squirrels or the hot pursuit of villains.

I knew her feel for dangerous situations was keen and I trusted her as a barometer as much as my other senses. She would not cavalierly approach the porch if she sensed danger. After again surveying the grounds surrounding the house, I made it to the side of the front door in about three giant steps.

I called several more times and knocked loudly with my left hand, still keeping the gun aloft.

The silence alarmed me and I had a picture of Eva, unconscious for lack of medication, lying on the floor inside. I ducked the door window and moved to the hinge side of the door. I grasped the old metal doorknob and swung the door wide; my right arm following the swing around till I was facing the kitchen, arms outstretched, both hands clasping the .38 in a classic firing stance. Tension laden situation or not, it was a move that repeatedly made we want to do my best Policewoman Angie Dickerson impression and say, "Freeze you turkey!"

As I lowered the gun and my arms, I am sure, like some syncopated swim move, my jaw must have sunk at the same time.

The kitchen was empty of furniture or belongings. There was nothing there but gray-white walls and the aging linoleum floor. The house was as bare as if it hadn't been occupied in years.

CHAPTER FIFTEEN

The entire house was empty. No Eva, no furniture, nothing. It had not been a home crowded with frivolous belongings, but this was an abandoned home. It looked so long empty that you could almost imagine rodent waste in the corners, but the floors and walls had been swept and washed. I moved down the hall to see if the rest of the house was as devoid of human presence. Every room was the same. Even the day-glo riot of music posters in Charles' room were gone.

What the hell had happened? Either everything in this place had been beamed up by the Starship Enterprise, or I was having some kind of mental collapse. Just as I was beginning to run myself through a personal sanity check, I received the tether I needed.

There on the chipped beige door of Charles forbidden room, was the gouge Eva and the grocery boy had made breaching the inner sanctum.

I headed back out the front door and stood in the driveway. How in the hell had all of this been packed and carted off in such a short time? It would have taken a fairly large moving van and all night to do it. Eva had certainly not been in any shape to pull it off so thoroughly. Hoover was still crisscross tracking the yard. I squatted down to check for car tracks and saw where a large vehicle had been backed to the front door. From the look of the tracks it had been some kind of trailer with multiple wheels.

"*Probably something like a horse trailer,*" I thought, and then I froze.

Had I seen the trailer that had emptied this house when I left last night? Had that been Charles that I had nearly t-boned out at the highway? It would explain why the rig had roared off so abruptly when I started to get out. If Eva's account of Charles' over-protective nature were correct, he would have been startled to see anyone exiting his private access road. Had he come back after I left to cover his tracks?

Eva's panicked sense that Charles had returned may have been dead on. Given my concern for Eva, or Mary, I then hoped that was not an unfortunate or descriptive thought.

I headed off down the road at a jog. I would need to let Dan call for the help that would start the crime scene process of the house. Bare as it was, there might be something to provide a clue as to where they had gone. Through the rather heavy recriminations I was busy stacking on my psyche for not registering a Charlie alarm, or for not at least forcing Eva to come to town with me, I was sending up a powerful prayer.

"Please Lord, let this woman still remain a victim of abduction, and not some fate far more complicated or sinister."

I spent more time than I wanted with the crew at the scene of what had been Mary Milton's last known address. I suspected that fingerprints would be tough to come by. The house had every indication of having been sterilized. The fact that the evacuation had been done so quickly, however, gave some promise of success. I went over everything I knew for the officers in charge. I had only been in the kitchen, the hallway and Charles' room, so I was unable to tell them what had been situated or moved from the rest of the house.

Eventually, Sheriff Mickey and I headed back to town. On the drive, we again mentally walked through the small framework of information that I had accumulated.

There was the Carl who delivered groceries to look for; there were the filed receipts that had been in Charles' room referencing Union, Cascade Locks and Portland. Unfortunately, being interrupted during my search of those files had kept my reference information at a minimum. If Charles was 'out there' doing his work for long periods of time, the potential existed that he had other places to hang his hat. Could Charles have transferred everything in this house to either of those areas?

I had no idea if the fact that Eva-Mary had called me in was the reason for the abrupt exodus, but I had a good sense that it was. The presence of someone who could blow the whistle on Charles, the missing Mary or the possibility of criminal abduction would send any 'normal' criminal fellow around the bend, or at least down the road.

We stopped in the town of Union to inquire around about the reclusive couple up the creek. Apparently they had been such loners, and their house so remote, that most people hadn't been aware folks had been living out there.

Neither the hardware nor the two small grocery stores had a deliveryman named Carl. No one recognized Charles or Eva from the small picture that I had fortunately lifted from the house before all of the rest of the contents had disappeared. It was one item that had unwittingly and hopefully unknowingly, been left behind. We walked up and down Union's Main Street, showing their picture in the drug store, the bar and grill, the video rental store and the restaurant in the old, restored Union Hotel. Apparently Charles had not spent time supporting the retail section of the town. The picture produced no spark of recognition. This had been consistent with the reports from the local Union police. Their arrival with the county sheriff's crew at Charles and Eva's house had been the first visit they had paid to that now ghostly empty home up Catherine Creek. There were likewise no names recorded to receive mail at the post office. Apparently lives lived off the grid can provide a sufficient hideout.

We headed back to La Grande and made a stop by the Alder Street Market to try and trace any regular delivery employees that they might have named Carl. It was a favorite of mine, a small neighborhood store with a sort of cosmopolitan feel. It was unique enough to successfully keep a good customer flow despite competition from the chains. There was a genuine meat department that would cut to specifications, a bakery that would draw you in for blocks around and they also sold fresh cut and potted flowers in an outdoor area during the good weather months. The market had not heard of Carl, nor did they provide any delivery service to the outlying areas. I showed the market owner the small photo. Neither Mary Milton, nor her husband Charles, rang his recognition bells.

Dan took the photo of Charles and Mary for copying and distribution, promising to return it to me later in the day. He dropped Hoover and I at my truck and promised to get me information as soon as he had it. He was going to forward the picture to both the Hood River and Multnomah County Sheriff's offices, mother counties to Cascade Locks and Portland, as well as all jurisdictions in between. The State Police had been alerted to watch along the freeway for a horse trailer being utilized as a moving van.

I headed straight home to throw traveling supplies in Sam the truck. There were only two places I could think to go looking. Cascade Locks or Portland. They were both in the same direction and, of the two choices; Cascade Locks would provide a much smaller haystack.

It was a plan and I needed to be doing something fast. I knew I would need to be clear-headed, so I worked at controlling anger born of frustration and guilt. I had not just misplaced a client. I had failed a victim who had been lost long before I had even met her. I had not taken conditions seriously enough, and because of that, Mary Milton's situation was compromised even further than it had been. It made me absolutely determined to recover her.

I packed for independent living on the cheap. This investigation was obviously going to be on my nickel, I had lost my client, but it would be my gift to Mary. Hopefully she would still be alive to appreciate it.

CHAPTER SIXTEEN

I filled Sam with a canvas overnight bag I kept packed for quick departures, a sleeping bag, a small, hard shell ice chest and extra ammunition. I called Bill Peterson, my lawyer landlord. His wife Maggie answered and she invited me over for barbeque later in the day. I graciously declined, letting her know that the only thing that could possibly make me miss one of her cookouts was the fact I would be gone for a couple of days. I then asked for her services at mail and paper retrieval. She repeated her always-open invitation to have Hoover sleep over at their house in my absence.

I laughed and said, "Now Maggie, that's not possible, you know I need someone to spell me driving."

Maggie and Bill Peterson, like Sheriff Mickey and his wife Elaine were good friends and surrogate parents. They fuss and spoil Hoover and I like we are their own. Unlike the Mickey's large, extended family, Bill and Maggie were childless, so having us on the grounds provided them all the benefits of children to spoil and none of the parental angst. They are an endearing couple whose polar opposite personalities completely compliment each other.

Bill is as deep and calm as a windless sea. The legal profession he had chosen was a better industry for his participation. I had watched him in action in the courtroom on numerous occasions and he could be as fierce and ruthless in the defense of his client as a mother bear over a threatened cub.

It was truly awesome to watch.

He has a very endearing side that causes him, at parties, after his absolute two-drink limit, to recite Robert Burns or Robert Service poems with the skill of a London stage actor. Sharing the 'precious words of the Robbies' he called it. I know that small slice of theatrical practice was an integral part of his courtroom dramatics and his friends always settle when he begins, never tiring of the familiar performance.

In contrast, Maggie is a tiny whirling dervish. She is involved in nearly every civic function in the community that needs a helping hand. She builds houses for Habitat, she chairs fundraisers at the hospital, she reads to children at the library and she helps the Red Cross raise funds and hold blood drives. She has a salt and pepper pixie cut and more energy than five women her size.

She is also an experimental chef and keeps my refrigerator full of, sometimes unrecognizable, offerings. Hoover has been sworn to secrecy as to how many we rapidly recycle.

As Maggie went off to find her husband, I ran a brief on-line white page phone listing and address check of Cascade Locks. The small population made the search brief, but with only first names to go by it was a wild stab. Given the remote, off-the-grid existence that I had encountered up Catherine Creek, old Charlie probably wouldn't be advertising his name, if that truly was his name, or even if he had phone service. The mobile, cellular phone industry has changed the way that we do business, and nowhere is that more prevalent than in the shady world of those who don't choose to leave a Hansel and Gretel path behind them.

Although the city search of Union had proved fruitless, I had hopes that the town of Cascade Locks' small size would offer the advantage of someone potentially having at least seen our Charlie's face in passing.

Bill came on the line and I gave him a brief run-down of my last 24 hours. He said he remembered the Miltons and the case of their daughter's disappearance, but he hadn't heard a word about them in years.

I knew Sheriff Mickey would be trying to locate the Miltons, but I also knew that having more than one set of ears to the ground often brought different and useful tidbits. Bill cautioned me, as he usually did, made me promise to check in and rang off saying he would inquire among others who had known Dr. Milton and his family to see if he could turn up anything that might help.

The news records reported she had been taking some classes at the local college. I followed my call to Bill with one to Richard, a fellow in the college-now University's administration office that I occasionally date.

We have a no pressure, no ties friendship that suits us both. He is once divorced, once widowed and we both are comfortable in a slightly better than mere friends relationship. We share a passion for cooking gourmet ethnic foods and renting new release videos as an excuse to eat king-sized amounts of buttered popcorn. He is kind, nice looking and he spoils Hoover.

She tolerates sharing me but enjoys his company as well.

"I am trying to run down a former student's transcripts or a list of long past professors in the art and theatre department," I told him after we had exchanged the usual, warm chatter.

"Well, you're a lucky girl today", he said in a very, bad imitation Irish brogue, "it just so happens that our alumni association has been putting together a memorial piece on past educators. Some are gone but t'will now not be forgotten thanks to their efforts."

"You are so good at what you do and a prince to boot."

It was an honest compliment. He was both.

"As far as the student info," he explained, "that gets privacy complicated and requires a bit of paperwork."

"I haven't the time for process," I explained, "Just shoot me the teacher names, if you would, kind sir."

He left the line to collect the information. When he returned, I gave him the year that Mary had spent time as a student and he gave me the names of the only two arts educators that were still alive. As my Irish luck held, one of the two still maintained a local residence. The other had retired to the big Island of Hawaii.

"Elisabeth King is just a pistol," he laughed. "She taught sculpting, painting and some theatre arts until 1982. She still periodically shows up at faculty reunions. I understand she was constantly at odds with administration and the community regarding her production choices. She was a young teacher, and was constantly pushing for change."

"What kind of change?" I asked.

"Oh, I don't know, employee policies and procedures, cause of the day stuff."

I told him I needed to get on the road, blessed him and his efforts and rang off, promising to call when I got back to town. I was anxious to be off in what I hoped was a direction of hot pursuit, but I was still feeling a need to expand on my 'Eva-Mary' file.

I decided to see if Professor King had a few moments for me. There was a listing in the book for E. King. In a town this size, there were only about ten Kings, and there was only one 'E'. I dialed and she picked up on the second ring. She had a husky, cigarette alto, and she pronounced all of her syllables. She could have sought employment in the recorded message industry.

I identified myself, established her as the professor I sought and explained I needed to talk to her about a potential former student but was on my way out of town. She agreed to see me right away, so I loaded the last of my trip essentials, music and snack food, and drove Hoover and I to the address she had furnished.

The south hill address was among those of other affluent professional residents of the city. Sturdy, older craftsman homes mixed with angular modules of more recent architectural styles that housed the city's medical, legal and educational population. Elisabeth King's home was spare and unadorned. A simple and fastidiously maintained yard fronted a dark gray slab of a house.

She opened the wide front door dressed in a floor length Indian style sari of rose and pale blue. Her short, once-black hair stood up in shiny wet, gray spikes. She was thin and the hand she extended had unbelievable long, bone thin fingers. She had to be in her late sixties to mid seventies, but she had aged very well. She looked about fifty.

The outside simplicity of her home was carried throughout the inside as well. She escorted me through, toward a kitchenette-dining area that overlooked a patio area. A complex, oriental-looking, canvas umbrella provided shade over an outdoor seating arrangement.

Spare modern furniture, mostly chrome and pale leather. Small abstract paintings, as well as black and white photocompositions, were almost swallowed up by large expanses of bare wall in odd colors of peach and pale mustard.

I had sort of expected her walls to be heavily adorned with big excessive paintings. They were not. No signed playbills or framed production advertising spoke of a lifetime of teaching the craft of art and drama. Maybe so many bad student art projects caused her to simplify her surroundings. Simplicity brought on by a life of visual overload.

As unadorned as her personal space was, everything about her personal carriage and demeanor spoke fine arts.

"You must pardon my appearance," she enunciated beautifully. "I was gardening when you phoned and

I took a moment to clean up before my company arrived."

She sat me at the glass kitchen table, produced a tray that held a coffee carafe, two cups, cream, sugar and tiny spoons. She managed the whole procedure without ever once turning her back on me, her audience.

"I hope this isn't such a horrible intrusion," I again apologized. "I am trying to locate someone, a Mary Milton, and I understand she might have been briefly a student of yours a long time back."

She paused at the name, frowned and tilted her head to match the name with year upon year of endless class rosters.

"The missing girl?" she stopped when the roulette wheel of her memory found its winning slot. "It has been such a long time since I heard the name. Goodness, that was a long time ago. Did she never turn up?"

"She may have, briefly, and I am just trying to verify that it was her. Her parents aren't here anymore and you may be the only one left in this town that had any real interaction with her. I was hoping you might have some recollections or insights into her disappearance that might help me. So, she was one of your students?"

"Very briefly, as you probably know. She would naturally stand out though, because of the curiosity of her disappearance, and the uproar it caused. As I recall she was very lovely, and showed great promise. A perceptive painter and she showed some acting promise. In the short time she was here, I believe she was being tapped for a lead. You say she has not turned up until now? How very sad."

"Sad, yes, but there may be reasons that have kept her from surfacing. That is what I am attempting to find out. Did she talk about herself at all with you?"

"I do remember the police coming to the school at the time of her disappearance to question the faculty and students. That was of course a poor time for student and police interaction. I remember that caused quite a stir. I don't think she was so very different from the other students of the day, all given to dressing down, wearing beads and listening to music that confused and angered their parents. Rather like every new generation, when you really think about it."

"Nothing stands out, at all?"

"Well, she had more sophistication I suppose, she had a certain presence. I think she was brought up in a larger community, had wealth and, if I remember correctly, had been off living the life of a carefree California flower child for some time."

Professor King was in mid soliloquy and I let her wander through her memory.

"It gave her a certain cachet with the less experienced students. I suppose they did treat her with deference. She was quite an art student. Gifted perhaps. She was quiet. She held back a lot about herself. I don't know if that was from needing to hide painful things, drug experimentation or just shyness. I personally rather like reserve in a student. A bare emotional canvas accepts the color of new characters far more successfully."

She said that last sentence like it was Shakespeare.

I guessed it wasn't.

I found her a bit formal and cold. The whole students as vessels to be filled, not figured out, or emotionally assisted, made me glad she had not been one of my teachers.

"Were you or any of her classmates able to help the police at all when she went missing?" There was always the slim chance that Mary could have left a few unintentional direction markers with someone.

"No, as I said, she tended to hold her personal life back." She cocked her head as if the action might serve to ratchet more memories to the surface. "There was one young girl who seemed to latch on to Mary. Almost idolized her a bit. A rather quiet girl, from the Pendleton area I believe. She was devastated by Mary's disappearance, grew very distraught, spent hours of her own time searching for Mary. I believe her name was Beth, Beth Miller or Mueller. Not an outstanding theatre student, a bit plodding and ordinary as I recall. In fact I don't remember seeing much of her after the whole Mary-missing person's incident died down."

The road called to me. Again, I thought how fortunate I was that Professor King had not been someone I looked to for inspiration. She seemed possessed of a cold edge, or maybe she was just a victim of the retirement 'sours'. The good professor appeared to be at the end of her Mary Milton Memory Lane, so I excused myself, thanking her for seeing me so quickly. I gave her a card with my numbers in case anything else sprung to mind.

"That whole era seems so long ago," she mused, still lost in thought, "so much time has passed and so much has happened since then."

"More to some than to others." I remarked, leaving the quiet simplicity of gardening and introspection that this woman had retired to. I placed a second call to Richard in Admissions and wheedled him into checking the alumni files for a Beth Miller or Mueller who might have been a student during the Milton incident. I really needed to know if she was still in the Pendleton area and my hope was that she had remained a participant of alumni activities. I hoped the alumni lists would not require the kind of privacy wrangling that the old student lists required. Without my having to provide too much detail, the urgency in my voice bought Richard's cooperation. He told me to give him a half-hour or so and I said I couldn't wait, but would call him from the road.

I gassed up Sam at the Exxon station out on the strip and stopped by the Sheriff's office to retrieve the picture of Charles and Mary Milton. It was the only real solid connection I had to Mary and it seemed to be the only tangible connection I had. The Sheriff was out. I left him a message that I was headed out of town for a couple of days, but would have my cell phone with me.

Cell phone service in the mountains and gorges of Oregon is a patchwork grid of unreliability. The general expectation is that if you are in an area where you need to call out in an emergency, your cell window will read *'No Service Area'*.

Nevertheless, I kept mine charged and handy.

I hit the I-84 freeway around 3:30 expecting to reach the Columbia Gorge town of Cascade Locks at about dark. It would be four-lane most of the way and spring weather usually guaranteed the passes wouldn't be closed or clogged with snow. I planned to call Richard back, once I had made it through the mountain pass and was nearer Pendleton. If Mary's shadow Beth was a local girl and was traceable, I might still be able to find her and connect on my way through. It would put me into Cascade Locks later than I wanted, but at this point any information was worth a brief detour. As it was, I was headed off pell-mell in a direction I hoped was correct, following the non-existent trail of a woman who for all I knew may not be around to appreciate my frantic pursuit.

Well, at least I had a plan.

Hoover sat on the far edge of the bench seat, the wind from the partially opened window flapping her half-open mouth into a doggy grin. She looked blissfully happy. She was. My canvas bag in the truck indicated some kind of a journey and she anticipated distance trips with the glee of a promised grade school vacation to Disneyland.

We barreled along, over Meacham pass, cruising the corridor of tall pines and enjoying the hazy, distant, purple mountaintops. The freeway is usually a slalom course of 18-wheeler trucks; most struggling to gear up or down respective of the many inclines or steep descents. In winter the pass becomes a life and death driving struggle when ice and snow complicate matters for our truck driver friends from the southern states who either don't want to stop and chain up or think they are skilled enough to disregard the blinking billboard warning signs. Three or four jack-knifed trailer rigs and you have traffic backed up to the Idaho border.

Today however was a beautiful spring afternoon and we made good time, weaving our way in between various big rigs. I had the speakers up loud and the player was alternating between Springsteen's, Darkness on the Edge of Town, a Celtic compilation and a favorite Pirates of the Mississippi CD. I sang loudly. It makes the miles fly by. Hoover eventually circled a comfortable spot on the seat and slept in spite of my singing. That also makes the miles fly by.

A soon as I was in cell range I phoned Richard. The good luck fairies were obviously hovering near my corner today.

Beth Mueller, was an active alumni, was still a Mueller and indeed still lived in Pendleton. She was listed as having a gift shop called NATURAL-LY located on a side street right off Main Street. I thanked him profusely, promised to reward his efforts upon my hopefully triumphant return with a reprise of a particular Thai chicken dinner he had raved about some time back.

"Your company would be more than enough," he said with a laugh "but that really was exceptional Thai chicken."

CHAPTER SEVENTEEN

I pulled Sam off the freeway at the first Pendleton exit, and wove my way down the hill into the core of the downtown section. The Pendleton Round-Up fills this city each September with rodeo cowboys and girls as well as several thousand other people in boots and hats who only wish they were reckless enough to strap themselves to the back of big, frisky, snorting animals.

It is also one of those annual events where people come to party. Many non-Wrangler local residents abandon their town and take that week off to go elsewhere. I suspect they head off to places where some of them can go party anonymously in someone else's town.

It has been happening just this way for a century. If you are a retailer, that many visitors to town is like winning the September sweepstakes. There are lots of opportunities for spending excess cowboy dollars in the shopping district of downtown Pendleton and I expected that Beth Mueller's shop would be one that was a beneficiary of some of those annual Let 'er Bucks.

I pulled up in front and rolled the windows down all the way for Hoover. The spring and summer heat in this section of eastern Oregon can make jerky out of your beloved pets quicker than you can say, "Man, I thought I left that window cracked open a bit."

NATURAL-LY was a remodeled store front that I had remembered at one time being a flower shop. The front window was arranged attractively. The script on the window indicated that the merchandise featured cotton and linen clothing, handmade soaps, lotions and high-end local crafts.

Call me a dumb old girl, but I love this stuff.

I pushed open the front door and a bell tinkled toward the back. The interior of the shop was cool after the warm spring afternoon. There was a clean grassy, linen smell with just a hint of lemon and lavender. It was a lovely store, packed with products that reflected its name; natural based products and comfortable clothing just like the window indicated. Not a great deal of polyester, nor was there an abundance of rodeo paraphernalia here. It was a bit of an oasis.

From the back of the store came a tall, broad shouldered woman with her hands full of woven wheat wreaths. These are locally generated, intricately woven decorations that reflect the agricultural strength of the region. A naturally beautiful bi-product from the nation's breadbasket.

"Hey there, can I help you?" she asked. She had moved behind the counter and was attaching the wreaths to a display rack.

"I really hope you can. Are you Beth Mueller?" I asked.

She looked at the investigator license I was holding out, glanced down at the woven wheat in her hand and let out a big gal laugh.

"It's only wheat straw, nothing stronger here. If you are working with the police, I quit messing with other grasses decades ago." She said it with the humor of someone who is very comfortable joking about themselves and their surroundings. She was still smiling broadly.

She was in her fifties. She wore no make-up and had the kind of tanned, freckled skin that spoke of riding horses and outdoor ranch work. Very simple, and natural. Like her store.

I liked her.

"No, I am a private investigator working on a missing persons case. It turns out this is someone you might have known."

"Somebody local?" she asked, leaning broad arms on the glass counter top.

"Not really, at least not any more and not officially," I said. "I got your name from an old Eastern professor of yours, an Elisabeth King. It is in regards to a woman you may have known back in college."

"Mary!" it was one word and it exploded out of her like a shot.

"Professor King said you might remember her."

"I knew it, I knew it! I absolutely knew she would turn up." Beth smacked her had down on the counter top for emphasis. "Finally, someone is going believe me."

I hadn't expected this much reaction, but I remembered the good professor saying Beth had taken the disappearance hard. I was willing to milk her enthusiasm for all it was worth.

"As I understand, it you were pretty close to Mary when you had classes together. Professor King said you had tried to assist the police at the time of her disappearance and I hoped you could fill me in with anything you might remember."

"Is she back in La Grande? Is she safe?"

"Well, I'm not sure."

There was no sense making her worry about whether Mary had turned up only to have potentially really disappeared permanently.

"I believe I may have seen her yesterday," I continued. "The trouble is, she is missing again and I am actually on my way down the gorge to follow a lead to see if I can find her."

"Well, the bright elusive butterfly. Where did she turn up this time?" asked Beth, one eyebrow raised.

"This time?" I asked, not exactly sure what she meant.

"Well, yeah. I saw her at an outdoor, folk concert up in Washington about ten years ago."

CHAPTER EIGHTEEN

I had to have looked as floored as I felt.

"Are you sure it was her?" I finally managed to ask.

"Until just now, I wasn't really sure. At the time, I thought it was her, but it had been since college when I had seen her last. I tell you I just about freaked out. But, then when I called out to her, she didn't turn around and then this guy she was with hustled her off like a house on fire. I figured I had made a mistake and then I kind of got a little embarrassed. I didn't follow them any farther, but I thought about it a lot later. It really looked like Mary, only older."

"Have you got time to sit and have coffee or something?" I was feeling the need to sit and think this through. I had too many questions for an over the counter chat.

"If this news doesn't rate a break time, I don't know what would." Beth moved around the counter and flipped the 'I'll be back sign' in the window.

"Let me grab my bag. We can walk down the street and get something at the coffee shop."

The coffee shop had some quiet tables in the back and we settled in with thick, white mugs of dark coffee. Beth wrapped wide, solid hands around her mug and stared down into the liquid. She kept shaking her head saying what a 'flash from the past' this all was.

She was not the mental picture I had formed of a fawning lackey to Mary the gifted, rich girl. This was a confident business owner with a sense of humor and of herself. From the passing conversations she had with other people we had passed, she was liked and respected here. Of course she had a few years between then and now to evolve and I was only basing my pre-judgement on Elisabeth King's assessment.

Leave it to the good professor to overlook a little human potential.

After establishing that one brief glimpse of a person she 'thought" was Mary had been the only connection she had had since the disappearance, I asked her to take me back to their school time together.

"What I need you to do is tell me everything you remember about Mary and all of the things she told you about her old school and California. Things like did she talk about the commune? Did she have a specific boyfriend? Plans for the future?"

"Whoa," said Beth. "Remember this was a while back, and it was the 60's. I was there. I'm not supposed to remember any of it."

She smiled and settled back in the wooden chair. I took out my red notebook and wrote as quickly as she spoke.

According to Beth, the Professor's take on Mary had been truer to form. She was pretty distant most of the time.

"I always figured some of that came from that de-programming crap her parents put her through. That was pretty rough, but back then parents were really flippin' out. The whole hippie movement scared their suburban socks off."

"Did she talk about her parents much?" I asked.

There is always room for Freud.

"Ah, she hated 'em. But everyone did back then. I don't know, maybe kids still do now. It just seemed like at that time the generation gap was really getting wide. Flower children wrote the book on parental shock value."

"Maybe since that generation is now grown and are parents or even grandparents themselves, they are less apt to suffer that magnitude of confusion when their own kids and grandkids are looking for the next new rebellion," I ventured.

"Oh yes," and the good book sayeth, the sins of the children shall be visited right back on 'ya."

"Did she talk much about the commune in California?"

Beth thought for a bit and then said, "Not much. But then her folks had just spent a lot of their good old money getting her to forget all about that section of her recent past. I know there had been enough drug use that she was familiar with most of the garden varieties circulating. I don't think she got that information from watching dear old dad at work."

"You mean she was still using?"

"Nah, I think she really wanted to be in control of herself. I don't think she ever felt like she was. People seemed to always be trying to take charge of her. Her folks, the teachers, Bobby."

"Bobby?" I asked, raising my head up from my notes.

"Yeah, Bobby. He was the guy she had been California dreamin' with. He was the one she had picked up with back east. He's also the one that hustled her out to the sunny shores of the West Coast."

"Did she miss him or talk about him much?" I figured Beth would have heard more about boy friends than her parents would have heard and reported.

"Some, but Mary was not a gushy, boy-chatty kind of girl. Mostly she just said he was older and from what I gathered, pretty mean and bossy. He also cheated on her all the time. She didn't date any of the local guys. Said all she wanted to do was 'her thing', not what everybody told her she had to do."

"Do you think there is the possibility the de-programming was less successful than her parents thought and she ran away to join up with him again?"

"No, well…. I don't know. She wasn't like pining away for him or the people in California. At the time, when she disappeared, I would have bet money she was dead. I always thought someone came off the freeway, saw a beautiful girl and grabbed her. I mean she just dropped off the face of the world too suddenly and besides, we had plans. We were going to study for a final together the night she vanished. We'd been planning a shopping trip to Boise the next weekend and we had even talked some about finishing up at Eastern, then rooming together in Eugene to take some graduate classes at the U of O."

"Do you think her boyfriend Bobby would have come up to Oregon and retrieved her, willingly or not?"

I still wasn't feeling any closer to getting a handle on the whys and where's of Mary's disappearing act.

Alien abduction was going to be my next question.

"I really don't know," Beth frowned, "from what little she did say, he was pretty possessive, but he did have plenty of female companions to choose from, even when she was with him. I gather her father laid down some pretty meaningful threats when he came swooping down to California to get her. Daddy could be quite a force as I remember. Its no wonder she always felt a little bullied and overwhelmed by everyone."

I couldn't help but think how bullied and overwhelmed she had still seemed yesterday. I had read more than once that all too often, women who find themselves in abusive relationships are doomed to repeat the patterns that brought them to those situations. Was Mary a magnet for control freaks?

"So," I said, " if you've been thinking she was dead all these years, it must be a bit of a shock to discover she is probably alive and has been living nearby, at least part of the time anyway."

"It about half pisses me off," said Beth a bit sadly. "I spent a long time trying to find her myself. I spent years thinking the only thing that would turn up would be her dead body. If you have found her, and she has been around here, she could have at least have called me."

"Maybe, and maybe not," I said trying not to dwell on the dead body remark. "She may have wanted to, or even tried to, but it appears as though she has been a bit confused."

"Boy, so am I!" Beth rolled her eyes a bit and shook her head,

I asked her to tell me more about her friendship with Mary.

145

"It was so long ago and everyone's head was on a little backwards, but Mary was the first real girl friend I had even connected with. She was pretty, poised and sophisticated, but not in a stuck up way. She had these really hip clothes, she knew about cool music and I could talk to her about …. stuff. I suppose I might have been a bit envious. I was overweight, shy and had never really left home for any time at all and here was this gorgeous California blonde who could talk about Dylan and Donovan and had not only been to see the Dead, she had even smoked pot with them!"

"Did you ever see a picture of the boyfriend from California?" I asked.

"No, her parents wouldn't let her bring anything home from the commune, and I would guess that especially included any reminders of hippie boyfriends."

I reached in my bag and handed her the picture of Mary and Charles.

"Tell me, is that Mary, and have you ever seen that man before? "

"Oh yeah, on both counts," she said nodding, "and I would recognize her even today. I knew that was her, up in Washington that time…and that is the fellow who was giving her the bum's rush away from me when I called out her name."

CHAPTER NINETEEN

However much I was enjoying my visit with Beth, I was also feeling time constraints. There was a good chance that Charles was still giving Mary the 'bums rush' and I needed to catch up with the bum.

I exchanged phone numbers with Beth. She was not only a connection to Mary's past, but she was witty and we had a friendship bond forming already.

She wanted to come with me right then and do whatever she could to help.

"Now that I know she is alive," Beth sighed, 'I'm going to feel really frustrated just sitting here."

"Until I discover if I am even headed in the right direction this could be a wild goose chase," I said, still not correcting the 'she's still alive assumption', "and you have a business to run. The best thing you could do for Mary is keep some prayers in the air. "

"That I can do," she said earnestly. "For both you and Mary."

"Twice as good," I said smiling.

We shook hands and parted and I left with a promise to let her know if and when I found her dear, hopefully not departed friend.

The rest of the trip would take over three hours of freeway driving. It is a magically beautiful drive that I never tire of. It provides every landscape imaginable. The scenery changes often; from the tree-studded Blue Mountains I call home, down into the abundant wheat fields of Pendleton, past the dry, sandy, circle crop irrigated desert land where the freeway meets the Columbia River and down into the river gorge itself. The once water-buried canyons of 'the Gorge' offer rock formations that put sculptors to shame and waterfalls so frequent it appears that the mountains are leaking like a past-its-prime earthen dam.

The drive afforded me plenty of road time and my favorite end of daytime to puzzle over my new pile of information. Unlike the view around me, my puzzle kept coming up too many pieces short of a full panorama.

Obviously the situation included Charles having something to do with or at least knowledge of Mary's abduction. Did that connection stretch back to the California commune? It was a link to the colorful decade of Mary's notorious history, but maybe our Mary just favored outlaw types of the turbulent times. The wild posters in Charles' sanctuary meant he was either having a hard time letting go of his misspent youth or was trying to capture some sort of back to the past, retro 60's lifestyle. Why would he want to keep all that out of sight? Was he keeping Mary under-the-counter medicated? If so, how, why and with what? If he were keeping her down on the farm with pharmaceuticals, that might somehow explain her identity crisis and her apparent lethargy.

About an hour and a half into the trip my cell rang.

It was Dan Mickey. With the call, a few more of the puzzle fragments fell into place. The Catherine Creek house had turned up prints. The woodpile at the back had not been moved and behind the stack had been left an ax. There had been two sets of prints. One set matched the ones taken from Mary Milton's bedroom following her abduction. The second set came back attached to the name Robert Charles Jasper, as well as a number of variations on the same; Charles Roberts, Charles Jasper, Bobby Roberts, Jasper Charles and

Jack Charles. A boy with three first names; three interchangeable first names.

"That's getting close!" I almost said a bit loudly, making Hoover stir. Robert or Bobby. Beth had called Mary's commune boyfriend, Bobby. A common name to be sure, but what are the odds a simple gal could get tangled with two hippie Bobs?

Our boy Charlie-Bob's trail was fairly fresh. He had only two days ago been released from a Portland jail cell, where he had been languishing for three weeks, while authorities attempted to pin some fairly hefty drug trafficking charges to him.

Multnomah County, facing budget cuts, had been forced to matrix out, or in lay terms, release, some less violent prisoners. Robert Charles Jasper had been released. Back to the wilds of eastern Oregon. That might explain why he was late getting home to the potentially abducted little woman who was expecting him home from 'work'. Not exactly Harriet waiting to see how Ozzie's day was, but, dutifully expecting him home nonetheless.

Apparently, while in the city, our boy Charlie had happened upon a major undercover stakeout. Portland authorities had been trying to corral a network of unsavory twenty-something's; bad boys who had been hosting regular 'Raves' throughout the metropolitan area. Charlie had dropped by one of the residences in the process of it's being closed down by the boys in blue.

Our Charlie had been carrying way too many over-the-counter drugs for just a simple man. He claimed he had unfortunately had his wallet stolen the night before at a homeless shelter. He reported no permanent address, as he was on the move a lot, and had also found the large mixed bag of drugs he was in possession of, under one of the many bridges that span the Willamette River in Portland's downtown core.

"They said he put on a pretty good down and out story, and they didn't much believe him. He has got a list of priors that put him in the category of dispensing more chemicals than a chain drug store, but he is off probation, and has done his time. So, they let him and a lot of other bad boys out to make room for people they had more heartburn with."

Dan Mickey's voice registered a sarcasm that even the cell phone static didn't mask. "They figured he was bringing a bag of trick or treats for some upcoming Rave, but couldn't prove it."

"Mostly tricks, I'd wager." I said.

My brief encounter with Rave drugs of choice did nothing to quiet any concerns I had for Mary, and it hinted at what might have potentially have been keeping our girl down and out in the eastern Oregon hills.

"Considering Charles' commitment to drug supplies, we started bringing in a few of our more useful local informants for meaningful conversation," Dan happily reported. "They are virtually singing like the Tabernacle Choir. It turns out Charles had a couple of young front men around here that ran his errands."

"Does one of them happen to go by the name of Carl," I asked hopefully.

"Most of Charles' dealings he kept pretty close to the vest. These little lackeys were on a kind of need to know basis. The only one that ever had access to the place up the creek wasn't named Carl. We've pegged that one as a local troublemaker, by the name of Stevie Waters. Everyone calls him Stevie Wonder. We got him here at the station, holding him on driving for about the eight hundredth time with no license or insurance."

"What did he say about Mary?" I asked.

"He says he really only ever dealt with Charles and hadn't ever been inside the place or even talked to Charles' old lady until a week or so ago. He didn't even know if she was there half the time. She always stayed in the house when he was up there. That is until the last time he brought groceries up and that's when she came out all weird and shaky and asked him to help her."

"So Charles prevents the lackey from getting close enough to figure out her real identity," I mused.

"Makes sense, doesn't it?" said Dan, "Why old Charles was extra cautious about keeping her so isolated."

"Sure, if he is the one who took her, there was always the potential she could be recognized locally," I said, "Even by little stoner accomplices."

I started losing phone clarity in a canyon. I promised to call from Cascade Locks. My jigsaw puzzling had taken on a new aspect. Charlie's connection to the growing problem of kids, drugs and rock and roll.

CHAPTER TWENTY

Raves were the new Millennium version of the 'happenings' of the 1960's. Most were covertly advertised, usually by hand to hand posters that cryptically invited youth to abandoned buildings; buildings that Rave hosts rarely bothered to secure with rental agreement or landlord permission.

Habitually these orgies of loud trance music and underage substance abuse produced injury and had on several occasions resulted in death by overdose. Two years ago I had spent a couple of months investigating the disappearance and secret life of a young man at the request of his parents in eastern Washington. He had grown up working on his parent's wheat and cattle operation outside of Pullman. By all reports, he was a very nice young man. After graduation, he had pursued his aspirations of helping out the family farm operations by leaving to earn a business degree in the big city of Seattle.

His college years in Seattle had proved less academic than social.

He had begun, without permission, utilizing his parent's line of credit for a myriad of mysterious expenses. Tracing him had been an easy job. He had left a pathetically easy trail to follow.

It turned out the young man was basically living on the streets of Seattle, pawning whatever he could steal or purchase with his parents plastic in order to support an older woman, a promising drug habit and a collection of grunge music 'wannabe's' that he referred to as 'his band'.

They were remarkably awful. I tried to keep an open mind given the fact I didn't appreciate the style of music that they vainly aspired to. It was useless. They had no musical talent and even less good sense.

For some reason, known only to their substance abused brains, they had called themselves the Elliptical Caesars, but even those who counted themselves as part of the band's inner circle, referred to them as the Epileptic Seizures. The Caesar's main goal was to be a hit at Seattle Raves. They never did make it. Most of them ended up learning other skills in either juvenile detention or the Job Corp.

Through the course of tracking the young fellow down, I had become familiar and friendly with several of Seattle's lower strata, youth of today; another generation of counterculture youth and their aspirations. In a quick and curious turnabout of history, most of them wanted no more than to emulate their parent's hippie generation, which they seemed to be doing quite successfully.

With a few interesting variations.

On the whole, these kids' desires centered around getting high, experimenting with sex, locating new and interesting parts of their bodies to tattoo or pierce and gyrating to grunge and trance music. All of these cravings could be satisfied with wild abandon at frequently held, heavily attended clandestine Raves.

Boys and girls just wanna have fun.

Raves are, for kids, a grand scale version of inviting everyone over when your parents are gone. You are just asking to get busted. Pretty soon someone brings beer or drugs and the neighbors call the cops and it all ends up being not as much fun as you thought and potentially way more harmful than it was worth.

Big city Raves are enormous numbers of kids who do not necessarily know each other, drinking, dancing and consuming all kinds of drugs, from marijuana to methamphetamines.

Like any new fad, eventually someone finds out how to make a buck at it and then perverts and creeps find a way to twist the situation to their advantage.

The latest perversion of Raves is the prevalence of nasty substances like the date rape drug Rohypnol. Street named Ruffies; they turned out to be a sleep disorder drug that has been prescribed in Europe since the 70's. Supposedly unavailable in the U.S., like any other banned substance, it keeps appearing on American streets and in particular in the beverages consumed by unsuspecting young women who are out on the town. Its tranquilizing affect knocks girls out and allows predatory males access without acquiescence.

The young male stalker takes down the deer with the elephant gun. Happy hunting through chemicals.

Rave on.

I checked my watch, and was deciding if I had given my landlord Bill Peterson enough time to find a link to Mary's parents, when Bill called me.

He had successfully located some mutual friends in the medical community who had kept up a Christmas card relationship with the Miltons.

"The Doctor is the only one still alive. The mother died almost ten years ago. He must be in his late eighties now. They eventually ended up moving back east, near where Mary and her mother had attended college." Bill said. "The mother came from some money family. Not like Rockefeller money, but certainly able to hire things done. Apparently they never did really give up hope of finding Mary, although they did end up building and dedicating some theatre wing at the old alma mater in Mary's memory. That seems like some measure of resignation on their part and maybe acceptance of her probable fate. Apparently they established a rotating scholarship at the school for other girls who showed promise."

"And maybe a little better sense," I added.

"Lots of kids took some rocky paths in those days, Cate, and not all of them came out at the right destination." Bill mused. "I suspect that is true of all generations, but that whole Age of Aquarius group had a lot of issues coming at 'em from all sides. For some it ended up pretty mean and ugly."

"Seems like more 'rage' than Age of Aquarius," I suggested.

"There's a bit of the poet in you Cate," he laughed, "and that might be a safer line of work."

"Too many lost knights and damsels in distress to go literary," I said, with a touch of irony.

I pulled my notebook out of my pocket and I wrote down the phone number he had found for Dr. Milton back east. I rang off promising to give Hoover a good scratch for he and Maggie.

I did a bit of quick time zone calculations and decided there was no time like the present to make my introduction to Mary's doctor dad.

I pulled into a rest area that furnished travelers a pay phone and dialed the number that Bill had given me. It would be near bedtime back east and maybe past for an elderly man like Dr. Milton, but I weighed the situation and decided that it warranted disturbing his evening peace.

An efficient female voice answered the phone and crisply informed me that I had indeed reached the Milton residence.

I apologized for the lateness of my call, introduced myself and asked to speak to the doctor.

"Well, dear, I am his nurse-housekeeper and I generally hate to disturb him after he has settled in for the night."

"I do not mean to be a nuisance," I replied "but it is in regards to a family member and I believe he would want to take my call."

"Are you calling about his missing daughter too?"

"Have the police already been in touch?"

"Yes dear. They called from California a while ago and said they had nothing concrete yet, so I suggested they call back in the morning. He sleeps so badly anyway, this would merely serve to agitate him."

"Please don't take this wrong, but is the doctor still mentally alert and able to provide information that might help?"

"Sharp as a tack." she answered. "The mind is willing, sound like it is just the body that limits him."

"Then I understand your concern," I replied, "but I am currently in pursuit of his daughter's potential abductor and hopefully will be successful in locating his daughter. I need any information he can give me that might help. It may prove futile, or it may be a happy ending just like in the story books, but if his mind is alert, I would guess he is going to resent not having the chance to try to help."

I could almost hear her thinking over the phone line; the professional bull dog nurse giving in to either surrogate loving family concern or the potential of job preservation in case I was correct about the doctor resenting her interference.

"Will you promise to be as gentle with the news as you can?" Her voice was concerned. I chose to think it was for the good doctor.

"I do indeed," I assured her.

"I will need to stay in the room with him, just in case…" She ventured, her resolution to put me through starting to wobble a bit.

"I would certainly want you near for his support," I quickly assured her.

"All right," she conceded " I will need to put you on hold and transfer you into his room."

As I held the line waiting for her to connect me, I busied myself reading the various pen-scribbled declarations on the walls of the phone booth, marveling at the immaturity of young love that would post its affection here in public places or worse yet bathrooms. I love you so much I want our commitment immortalized in a toilet stall.

Not exactly sonnets, but passion transcribed for others to behold through the ages.

I also watched the interaction of the families who had stopped to use the rest area.

Dogs and children bounded out of the rear doors of cars and vans. Dads stretched themselves and moms set up temporary kitchens on the rough, scarred picnic tables or shepherded their squealing flocks into the relief facilities provided. Inland seagulls swooped the picnic area for morsels and echoed the shrieks of the excited children.

It all seemed so normal. A phone booth's eye view of an orderly world outside the glass. The goings and comings of American families on the move. Over the river and through the woods, vehicles packed with the anticipation of adventure and discovery. A protected universe, where, on the surface, there appeared no kidnappers, drug users or bad behaviors.

The line crackled slightly and the voice of an obviously older gentleman spoke.

"Hello, Mrs. Elder says this is concerning my Mary. Is she alive?"

"I believe she is Dr. Milton," I ventured, not knowing exactly where to start. I needed to feel him out and decide how best to approach him with and for information.

"But you are not sure?" he asked, reading more into my answer than I thought I had revealed.

"Mrs. Elder has probably cautioned you to spare me any undue stress," he continued. "That is her job - to protect my heart, but I assure you, any news you can bring me regarding Mary would be the best medicine for my faulty ticker. Be that good or bad news."

"She was correct," I told him. "You are sharp as a tack."

"I think I may have been holding on to my faculties for this very moment." he said, "Now, please tell me everything."

I did just that. I introduced myself and I told him everything I knew and some of what I suspected.

He made noises of acknowledgement periodically, but did not interrupt.

When I was finished, I turned the tables and said to him, "Now, can you add to or verify any of that information."

"What you have just told me verifies many suspicions I have always had," he began. "Mary's mother and I never believed she had run away. To us it seemed so convenient a solution for the police. Many children were leaving home then and it was, given Mary's previous behavior, all too natural to assume she had repeated her actions. But, we knew in our hearts that she would not abandon her home without a word. Even when she had been in that commune she had made some attempts to at least make us believe she was still back in school. In order to protect us."

"How did she do that, sir?" I interrupted.

She told my wife she had sent a few letters and postcards back to the campus to be mailed to us, but her roommate at the time had not been all that reliable. When our investigator showed up to inquire about our daughter's whereabouts, the girl panicked, not wanting to be implicated and burned all of the messages that she had been trusted to forward. It was one of Mary's biggest regrets, how much the whole affair had hurt her mother. They were very close. I am convinced she would not have turned right around and compounded that pain with a repeat of her actions."

"Did she talk about relationships she might have had with boys in the commune?"

"That was hardly a subject she and I would have been able to speak about." I could hear the generational disapproval mixed with parental embarrassment in his voice. Daddy's good little girl can't be pictured doing the nasty with young boys, especially worthless, subversive hippie boys.

"Would she have said anything to your wife ... about anyone at the commune that you may recall?"

"My wife and I spent years remembering everything, every word she ever spoke, Miss Conway, from her first childhood utterance to the last word she spoke to her mother on the day of her disappearance. If there had been anyone significant she had made reference to, I assure you we would have spared no expense tracking that lead."

"Do you recall the police reporting on a friend of your daughters named Robert or a Bobby or a Charles?"

"As I said, the police weren't exactly focused on Mary's return." His voice was slightly frosty but beginning to tire as well. I sensed I was losing his attention as well as his cooperation to the resentments he had built up over time. "She did not, nor could not, return to the commune, because there was no commune to return to. We had successfully scattered those mangy children to the four winds when we went down to retrieve our daughter."

"I had best let you try to rest," I said, "and I had better get back to searching for your daughter."

"I do thank you. It is odd to have this thread of hope after all of these years." His wistful, frail voice drifted off slightly and Mrs. Elder came on the line.

I left my number, in case he remembered anything else and rang off with the promise to report back as soon as I had any news.

As I drove toward the sunset of Oregon's western horizon I scanned my brain to bring up anything that I might be missing or hadn't thought through.

I also perused each horse trailer I passed for potential captives.

CHAPTER TWENTY-ONE

It was already dark enough for headlights when Hoover and I finally pulled into the small community of Cascade Locks. It is usually a fairly busy area, particularly with the pass through summer traffic, but it was relatively quiet on this cool, spring evening.

Cascade Locks used to be a main locks for barging river cargo and was also a once prosperous mill town in the heart of the Columbia River Gorge. Like other Oregon mill communities who lost their livelihoods and sense of place to radically misplaced and misrepresented environmental concerns, it has made a small name for itself harboring a paddlewheel boat that takes tourists out cruising up and down the Columbia River.

The town is small and constant, having remained structurally unchanged for decades. It is a freeway town that is often on the way to somewhere else, so the bulk of the six or seven-block commerce district is comprised of restaurants, motels and fueling opportunities. There is a school that, in the tradition of many small Oregon towns, provides all twelve grades an education together under one roof. It also has no established police force, just an infrequent patrol. Like the isolated, rural parts of eastern Oregon, it was another perfect place for under-the-radar-people like Charles.

The restaurants were filled with a few weary tourist families and the gas stations were closed for the night. There were no suspicious horse trailers on any of the streets I canvassed. I wandered into the only tavern that had any measurable clientele.

Like so many bars everywhere, it had the required dim overhead lighting, overly bright beer lights and heavily varathaned table tops. A stereo system provided music with too much bass and too little variety, through loudspeakers, placed too close to tables for intimate conversation. Like a cookie cutter Denny's restaurant or a Wal-Mart store, everywhere in the world you walk in one, it's just like being back home.

The woman tending to the liquor dispensing was falsely jovial and seemed a bit resentful that my arrival might require more work. An obvious honors graduate of Barmaid 101. She had a suspiciously brassy color of straw blonde hair, a good figure but poor teeth. Her tee shirt proclaimed, "If you don't like my peaches honey, try my melons."

I suspected more than a few of her regular patrons might be qualified and experienced fruit inspectors.

The potential harvest crew for the night turned up two guys engaged in a game of eight ball and one old fellow with his head resting solidly on his forearms. Neither the barmaid or the pool jockeys recognized the image I showed them of Charles and Mary, and the old fellow with his head at half mast had to close one eye to even locate the picture I held.

He said it looked a little like his parents.

One of the two hustlers decided that I had the potential of providing more sport than his current pool partner might. He began the mating dance of the cuckoo bar bird.

He had unfortunately consumed too many draft beers to successfully pull off the Cary Grant imitation he was attempting. If he hadn't been dead serious I would have doubled over laughing. It would have made for a spectacular Saturday Night Live routine.

I tried to calmly explain he would have a better shot at the number four ball, but he was fiercely determined in his beer-fueled quest. I made as graceful an exit as was possible.

As much as I hated to lose any more time, I decided to start fresh in the morning.

I would have to hope that after spending an entire night power moving out of his house, Charles might be needing rest as well, and that he would still be resting somewhere near here tomorrow.

Although I was set for camping, or, less luxuriously, sleeping in the truck, the onset of a not uncommon gorge torrential rain, and my later than I expected arrival, drove Hoover and I to a small motel called the Scenic Winds at the east end of town. It provided individual cabins, clean accommodations and a 'pets welcome' sign.

All the comforts of home.

I fed Hoover and then I called La Grande dispatch to leave the motel number for Dan Mickey. I figured he was probably off duty, but he was still at the station.

"Elaine finally kick you out so you have to pull up a cell bunk these days?" I asked, knowing that his wife

174

understood his level of commitment and generally expected him home when she saw him.

"I wanted to wait till the paperwork came in on your Mr. Charles," he said. "I went through the old Milton files and made some calls down to California. They had several hits for old Bobby Jasper, a.k.a. Bobby Roberts a.k.a. Bob Charles. Most of them several decades old, except for a couple of I-5 traffic infractions within the past five or six years. Seems he had a history of run-ins back in his youth with police. Pretty typical stuff for the time, frequenting drug houses, vagrancy, possession of less than an ounce, public intoxication. The more serious stuff started when he began associating with a troublesome organization that called itself Mother's Helpers."

"Bingo! This *has* to be Mary's Bobby!" I said it loud enough that a sleeping Hoover stirred at my feet. She opened one eye, assessed the danger level in the room, snuffed loudly, and then resumed her behind the eyelids squirrel pursuit.

"They investigated him pretty thoroughly at the time of Mary's disappearance. Reports had him pegged as her boyfriend at the commune, but he was shacked up with some other girl by the time she turned up missing, so they figured he was old news."

This was at least a fairly solid connection to Mary's disappearance, and a definite 'big' coincidence in the Bobby department. Charles was definitely linked to the merry California drugsters who had spirited Mary away from a promising education back east. She had to have talked about her folks and where they lived. He could have traced her to Oregon and taken her back from her parents. True love being what it was, the fact he was otherwise coupled again may not have meant he wouldn't have come looking for the girl that was so rudely taken away from his possession.

The fact that her father chose not to remember any references or reports about him in particular was probably an effort at memory cleanse on his part. A daughter is best remembered as a saint if there are no criminal element bad boys clouding history's picture.

There was no way of knowing if he had been the one who had taken her or if she had been kept in the same area for all of those years. If it had been him, it showed a certain level of arrogance on his part to have remained at the scene of the crime.

"What kind of priors did they turn up for Mother's Helpers?" I asked. I could hear Dan shuffling papers.

"Cop down there name of Richardson is gonna run a better report. Says this group, at one time, controlled a good chunk of the northern California cannabis trade. And it seems Mary wasn't the only girl that had frantic parents mounting a search party. Lots of young runaways reported and there were suspicions that some were supporting the communal family by trading favors on the mean streets."

"Prostitution?" I wondered out loud. "I thought that whole sexual revolution thing was about free love?"

"I suspect free didn't put much granola on the table", he said. "On top of that, the whole Manson family thing had everybody pretty spooked over large, communal groups of freaks, and the cops kept an eye on 'em, but every time they got to assembling enough reasons to bust them, they'd just pick up their tents and move on."

"The moveable beast," I said and wondered what had happened to the nomadic Mothers.

"I think that's 'feast,'" he countered.

"Don't get me started," I grumbled, "I haven't eaten dinner yet. Even the granola reference sounded good."

"Get some food and some sleep and I will get back to you as soon as I have anymore, and Cate…" his voice took on a combination father-superior officer tone. I find it exasperating, but endearing. "This guy is a rough character. He has a lot to answer for. He knows it and he probably knows we know some of it. Please be careful."

"You know I always am, *dad*." I reassured him jovially. Having someone worry about you is good. His seeing me as a sort of adopted daughter clouded his confidence in my ability to handle things at times, but it was a warm, fuzzy trade-off.

I decided to make my dinner the remaining yogurt and bananas that I had provisioned for myself on the trip down. Perhaps not all of the food groups represented, but it would mean early to bed, and early on the trail.

Long distance travel sedates me. I washed up and tucked myself into the utilitarian bed, pulled the blankets up and dozed off to the night sounds; waves of rain pouring over the side of the cabin and Hoover's sleepy dog snore.

CHAPTER TWENTY-TWO

For the second night in a row I did not sleep well. I rarely do in motels. Particularly when my brain keeps mulling over what I should be doing or figuring out. I kept jerking awake to check the clock, which moved in sluggish increments. The motel vacancy sign spewed an angry, red glow on the ceiling of my room.

If I were on a honeymoon or a much-anticipated vacation, I might have considered it a warm or sensual red. As it was, I had work to do. I also had the burden hanging over my head of missing the mark and not assisting a woman, a client, who was in danger. I was finding no comfort in trying to relax.

I was up, packed and looking for breakfast at one of the local cafes when they opened the door at eight. The coffee tasted like they had left it warming over night, but I had three cups to accompany a Spanish omelet, bacon and whole-wheat toast. I sat, reading the morning's Oregonian newspaper, waiting for the tables to fill.

Small freeway towns become used to the odd stranger in their midst, so casual interaction with the breakfast crowd at local restaurants is usually superficial, but cheerful and warm. It is, more importantly, filled with local information. If you want to know what goes on in a community, head to where the coffee or beer is consumed.

I had seated myself at the counter next to a back-to-nature looking couple who were laying siege to a couple of farmer-sized breakfasts.

Blue jeans and long hair do not automatically denote a lifestyle lived on the banks of the mainstream, but skin pallor and minimal eye contact speak volumes. Given the possible counterculture connection I was pursuing, they seemed a likely pair to warm up to.

Directly on the other side of me were a couple of older gentlemen in ball caps and similar wool, checkered jackets. It was obvious from their banter with the waitress that they were regulars.

The waitress was round and rosy and looked like a Disney fairy godmother. I had a fleeting wish that someone would get their order wrong to see if she would whisk out a wand and set things right. It was no wonder the two older gents probably made a daily habit of stopping by. She fussed over her customers like they were come-for-Sunday-company.

I happily joined their spirited conversation about weather, spring bedding plants and local high school athletics. It is a getting to know you mating dance that is the preparation for more in depth inquiry and it usually establishes a comfortable trust. Trust and large quantities of coffee, or more often alcohol, are the lubricants that make an investigation engine roar to life.

The younger longhairs to my left smiled periodically, but did not engage. They were apparently not regular enough to have made much of a familial connection with the jovial waitress. I decided to focus my attention on the two older gents.

Eventually the conversation evolved to inquiries about me and in which direction I was headed. It made me the one being investigated, which was to my advantage. Not deceptive, but a part of my learned chess moves toward discovery.

"I am actually on a long-lost family search," I said, producing the picture of Charles and Mary. "A cousin." I said, indicating Charles image. Of the two, his dark hair most resembled mine. He had to be someone's cousin. Still no real deception on my part. I have my scruples. I am unwilling to use up my 'thou shalt not lie chits' on anything other than self-preservation.

"I think he may have a place here in the Gorge somewhere, so, I am using a little vacation time trying to reconnect." Still on moral high ground. Without a paying client, I could, theoretically, be considered to be taking vacation time.

The ball-capped gentleman to my right glanced at the picture in my hand and then at me a couple of times before cautiously commenting,

"How long's it been since you seen that cousin?"

For a moment I thought my vagueness had not been convincing enough.

Then he continued, "If that's the fella I think it is, he's been into my station for gas and propane a number of times. Kind of a hard case."

Unsure of what name old Charlie would be using in these parts, and not wanting to show any alarm, I put on a face of happy discovery and asked, "You think it's him? Do you have any idea where he's living?"

"Don't know much, like who he is, or where he lives. He always pays in cash, but like I said, he's not the kind'a guy you bother with too many questions."

By now, I noticed curiosity had driven the counter-culture couple on the other side of me to lean in to look at the snapshot.

Their reaction was almost imperceptible, but I was ready for it.

The lank-haired younger fellow started slightly and glanced quickly at his female partner. I turned the photo to him and watched as he shook his head slightly and returned to his plate.

"I seen him in the grocery a time or two," this from the other older gentleman regular, "I think he lives down the old highway there out of Dodson."

The waitress, hair wisping out of a tight knot at the back of her head, a pot of regular coffee in one hand and decaf in the other, leaned over the counter to weigh in on the picture.

"Yeah, that fellow lives way back up behind the old Dodson store. Brought his wife in a time or two. Neither of 'em talks too much."

"His wife." I say trying not to sound startled.

It isn't a question really, but the round little waitress takes it as such.

"I think it was his wife. Pretty little dark-haired thing. Real quiet, skinny as a rail, always asking for no yolks in her omelet. Now, how in the world anyone can eat eggs like that is beyond me. Say, you folks want your bill? Well, thank you and have yourselves a nice day, now. Come on back soon."

I am processing the 'wife' information. I suddenly realize she is talking over my shoulder at the couple that had been seated next to me. They had quickly gathered their things, left a $20 bill on the counter and were out the door, the cowbell on the handle chiming, before her sentence was finished.

I stood, took a couple of pieces of bacon off my plate for Hoover and dropped a $10 bill on the counter. Haste was making for a lucrative tip day for our fairy godmother gal behind the counter.

I thanked the older gentleman for their assistance, asked again about the location being behind the Dodson store. They told me, their voices cautious without trying to insult what might be a relative.

I said I would make sure I dropped by for gas at my new acquaintance's station later. I made my way out the front door, down the steps and on to the sidewalk in time to see Bonnie and Clyde cruise by in an older model, blue hatch back Toyota.

They were not driving safely.

Both were watching me intently instead of the road. They seemed to be headed, as quickly as their elderly car would take them, toward Dodson. Apparently they wouldn't need to ask directions.

CHAPTER TWENTY-THREE

I had planned to make a couple of phone calls as soon as I left the restaurant. Faced with the imminent need to pursue the blue Toyota, I ignored all safety warnings and pulled out my cell phone while maneuvering the twists and turns of leaving the restaurant parking lot, down through town and out onto the freeway.

I passed under the toll span of the Bridge of the Gods at the western end of town. Local legend had it that a natural land bridge had once existed there connecting what is now the Oregon side of the Columbia River to Washington State. A sorrowful tale of unrequited love between a couple of local volcano gods had destroyed its existence.

Love is strange. It certainly can cause all sorts of damage.

I was still holding out hope that Charles had enough affection for his kidnapped wife that he wouldn't destroy her in his flight. What chance was

Mary going to have if it turned out he was keeping her in the mountains and some other little woman down here in the gorge? That may just equate to one wife too many.

I settled Sam into a respectful sixty mile an hour speed and positioned myself where I could see the blue Toyota about a quarter of a mile ahead of me on the freeway. I was pretty sure they did not know which car I would have gotten into to follow them, but again, Sam was not the best vehicle for anonymity.

I was approaching the freeway exit for the secondary road that would take me to Dodson.

I could barely see the blue Toyota. Here, off the freeway, I wanted to keep back a little farther. There was, however, enough blue exhaust pouring out the rear of their auto that even without a clear view of them, I would be able to trace their petroleum smoke signals. The waitress had said that Charles lived way up behind the Dodson store with his pretty, little dark haired wife. Sure enough, when I reached the abandoned old building that had once housed a restaurant and convenience market; there was a haze of blue smoke drifting sideways up the hill.

"Golly," I said out loud to Hoover, "Do you suppose these kids are so excited about me finding my long-lost cousin Charlie that they just want to be there to set up the reunion? Wonder why they didn't wait to guide me to him?"

I took the corner rapidly enough that Hoover slid sideways slightly on the seat. She righted herself and propped her paws on the dash staring at full attention out the windshield, her best, low 'look out you bad guys' growl filling the cab. The road forked about a half mile up and I knew there wasn't too much farther it could go, given the proximity of the mountain I was driving up toward. I swung Sam around and parked off to the side of the road facing downhill, again always cognitive about quick exits.

I took the .38 from its under-the-seat-compartment and slid it into my right jacket pocket. I kept my hand in the pocket and we headed up the heavily overgrown road following the trace of blue haze and the smell of under-utilized fuel.

Hoover automatically heeled to my left; our practiced move that kept her out of gun trajectory on my right side.

The dense undergrowth of this section of the Columbia Gorge is mind boggling, especially to the artists who regularly attempt to paint its scenic splendor. I had once hiked up a trail to one of the countless waterfalls that spews a combination of melting ice cave water and rain out of the wilds, down the sheer rock cliffs into the Columbia River system. Over a packed-in lunch I had sat in the overwhelming quiet and counted over ten, radically different shades of green. Someone had once remarked that the gorge actually was classified a sub-semi-tropical rain forest. Not as humid and warm as the jungles, but similarly chock full of thick vegetation and potentially dangerous animals.

Gorgeous scenery, but bad protective cover for stealthy pursuit.

The ferns, trees and root undergrowth were so dense I was forced to keep to the lane. I had taken advantage of several concealing bends in the road before everything opened out into a large cul de sac clearing. I rapidly moved to the side of an ancient, weather beaten garage and motioned Hoover down with my outstretched palm. Hoover was ready for my direction, and knew from my hand command that we were in silent mode.

The garage doors had long since been removed and the windows were devoid of all but a few corners of wavy, old glass. My position on the downhill side allowed me a fairly wide view of the surroundings through both the door and window openings.

There were three structures that appeared to be houses. The dampness of this area of the Pacific Northwest will eat an untended building faster than termites. The moisture from the ocean that doesn't get trapped by the coast range of mountains dumps out here at the foot of the Cascades. All three buildings in front of me were weathered and unkempt. The one closest was in the same shape as the garage I was using for cover. The lack of windowpanes and evidence of plant life taking an upper hand with the hinge-sprung door told me that it had been uninhabited for quite awhile.

In front of the next building was parked the old, blue Toyota, its engine still ticking in an effort at cooling. The female passenger of the Toyota was standing on the porch of the second house, half hidden in the doorway. She was watching the door of the third house intently, obviously unaware, to my great relief, that I was standing, watching, less than fifty feet behind her.

The door to the third house stood ajar. The white curtain on the front door window moved in the breeze, an indication that it probably had tenants. There was no vehicle parked out in front of the third house, but peeking out from behind the far side was the tail end of a gunmetal gray horse trailer.

CHAPTER TWENTY-FOUR

I had spent so much of the previous day looking for that trailer. If it wasn't the same one, it was an exact match to the one I had nearly collided with day before yesterday, down at the end of Mary's lane. It seemed odd to finally discover it here, up this remote road. But, this would be exactly where I would find it, an isolated location in a very sparsely populated area. A place removed enough to mask slippery, illegal and immoral activities.

The more than shady underside of the life's big rock.

I stayed behind the garage, waiting for Charles to come barreling out the front door with what was apparently his early warning system neighbor, but the only person who came back out was the long haired Toyota driver. He wasn't the kind of fellow who naturally sported a healthy skin tone, but he flew out the front door with a face as white as powdered coke. He was holding an old deer-hunting rifle across his chest. It looked like he had just grabbed it and he held it like someone unaccustomed to handling firearms.

He was breathing unevenly but managed to call to his female companion, "Get back in the car Nicki, Charlie and Angela ain't home and we gotta get outta here, now!"

Nicki began to protest in a whiney little girl voice, "Gary, she's just lookin' for her cousin. I keep tellin' you, it don't have nothin' to do with us. When Charlie gets back he'll make her go away. Quit being so damned paranoid!"

By now Gary had made it to his own porch and had grabbed hold of her arm trying to pull her toward their car, "No, its bad Nick, real bad. Charlie and Angela aren't anywhere in the house. The truck is gone, and something really bad happened. The furniture is all messed up and there is so much blood in the kitchen!"

At those words, I felt the weight of being too late.

I wanted to curse out loud at the news, but I was too close to them. The sharp snap of the screen door and their hurried scuffle steps down the walk told me I was about to lose these two to the open road. I stepped out; still half concealed by the side of the garage and pointed my gun directly at Gary's chest.

"Stop right there!" I said loudly. "Drop the rifle and raise your arms, up high! Both of you. Now!"

They did exactly what they were told to, stopping in the middle of the walk, halfway to the car. Gary almost threw the rifle to the ground; another inexperienced firearms move. He seemed like the kind who took directions, rather than gave them, but I was not going to take chances.

"Shit, she's a cop," said Nicki.

I let the observation stand. There was no sense quibbling over details when there was so much else that we needed to discuss. Particularly when everyone's adrenaline was so active.

"Who else is in your house?" I asked. I had not released Hoover yet and wanted to make sure we weren't going to have other longhairs to keep track of.

"Nobody, just us," said Gary. His eyes remained fixed on the gun barrel and his hands and voice were shaky with fear.

"Bring 'em out Hoover!" I commanded and gestured toward the house.

Hoover shot past Gary and Nicki at a low-slung run, like pent up water behind a floodgate. She had been waiting for this and she banged the screen door with her front feet hard enough to bounce it open. She then bolted inside through the opening she had created. The three of us waited outside while Hoover verified Gary's 'ain't nobody here but us chickens' claim.

Everything was very still. We could hear the click of dog toenails as she encountered spots of wood floor and linoleum through the small house. The only other sound was Gary's voice. He was mumbling to himself over and over in fear and dismay, "Shit, oh man, shit, oh dear."

Nicki remained quiet, her eyes wide as saucers. These kids were obviously users. They were probably not dealers, or at least not successful dealers, given their living quarters and the shape of their transportation.

But they knew Charlie, and they were going to help me find out where he was.

Hoover was back on the porch in a couple of minutes and I knew that the house had been swept more thoroughly than any human could.

"Now, up there!" I said pointing to the house that Gary had just emerged from. Potentially our Charlie's second home.

Hoover repeated her scan of the second residence with Gary, Nicki and I remaining quiet and still. It was so calm I could hear a train, half a mile or more down the hill, near the Columbia, it's wheels clacking on the rails. It sounded like a canyon echo of Hoover's toenails on the interior linoleum. Soon she emerged on the porch with her ears back and fur bristling. There was something wrong in the house, but it would not be someone or something that would cause me problems. I was confident there would not be anyone inside who was still alive.

Unless Charles had moved his truck away from this little compound and was hiding in the surrounding dense undercover, it was just these two I had to deal with. Big 'ifs', but my advantage grew as I eliminated each potential threat.

I positioned myself inside the old garage, feeling that if Charlie were somewhere near, the building would provide at least minimal shelter for my back. I kept the gun leveled on the hippie duo and my ear cocked for sounds surrounding us. I called Hoover back and ordered Gary and Nicki to walk between the Toyota, and me and to then stand in the middle of the cul de sac turn around. I wanted to make sure they did not try to get their old beater car in between us.

They stood quivering on the packed earth and old pine needle drive. Gary bleated, "Man, you ain't gonna shoot us are you? We didn't do nothin'. We just live here. We don't know nothin' about Charlie or drugs or nothin'."

Well, they obviously knew something, but this was his brain on drugs. I let him ramble and did nothing to reassure him that I wasn't going to plug them both dead there in the driveway.

There was no time or opportunity to search for ropes. I decided to use what was at hand.

"Now, one at a time, take off your clothes, make it quick," I ordered. "And do *not* try anything funny. That dog will take your throat out at my order."

The both glanced sideways at Hoover, who was watching them, her head down, neck outstretched and even with her shoulder blades. She punctuated my remarks with a low growl.

"You first," I indicated the girl, "get moving!"

"What?" squeaked Nicki, "I don't wan't .. I can't .."

"What are you doin' to us?" groaned Gary.

"Do what I tell you, and do it *very* quick. It is the best way to remain safe, I assure you!" I really like how at times like this I could pull off a very menacing, lower register voice.

Very authoritative and very impressive.

Lauren Bacall as Bogart.

It was working. Nicki was down to her underpants in seconds. She wore no bra, and probably didn't need to. She had a skinny, undernourished frame.

"You can stop there," I told her. "Now, hands back up!" She raised both her hands and stood with her knees slightly bent, as if hunkering down would cover her scantily clad body.

"You're next mister," I told Gary. I didn't need to. He was so pathetically eager to save his rear that he was shinnying out of his t-shirt and jeans; all the while apologizing for the embarrassing fact that he wasn't wearing underwear.

"I promise not to go wild with desire," I assured him, "now hurry!"

He finished and quickly raised his hands without my ordering him to do so. He crossed one leg slightly over the other as if to shield his private parts. He was a pale and sickly creature. I felt sorry for him, but not enough to be foolish.

"O.K.' I said, "You. Is it Nicki?"

She nodded, expecting the worst and shivering slightly.

"You are going to take his t-shirt and tear it into a couple of long strips and then you are going to tie his hands really tight behind his back with one of them. Can you do that without trying anything that will make me shoot you?"

She nodded again, then bent down and picked up his shirt from the pool of their clothing. The material, as worn and faded as it was wouldn't give at first, so she tore at it a bit with her front canine tooth. It then ripped easily, almost completely around with two jerks of her hands. When she had separated a long strip, I gestured for Gary to turn around and put his back toward her with his hands behind his back. This activity caused, for the first time, both of them to turn their backs slightly toward me.

On both of their right shoulders, slightly below the ridge of their shoulder bone they sported matching marks. Until now I had only read about the symbol in newspaper accounts and seen its fuzzy specter in the picture of Charles, but the image was obvious. I was close enough to see it was a round earth with two parallel lines running through it.

It was the group tattoo accepted and worn by the family of nomadic druggies that had sheltered and perhaps kidnapped Mary Milton.

Mother's Helpers.

These two were not old enough to have joined in the 1960's, so, apparently the communal opportunities and the wild and crazy drug years were still available for those interested in joining up. So much for Dr. Milton's declaration of disbanding the wild bunch. I wondered what other kind of hazing was required besides the body brand?

"Let's talk about those matching tattoos. What is that supposed to signify?"

I figured they might as well start supplying information while they worked.

"Charlie used to work in a parlor in the old days in California." Nicki volunteered. "He was a big time musician in California too. He has got a ton of cool tats. He put a really pretty butterfly on Angela's stomach. She said it didn't hurt all that much."

It was very difficult for Nicki to talk and work at the same time. She kept having to pause, to put her tongue in-between her teeth to concentrate.

She was, however, doing a bang up job wrapping Gary's hands together tight.

I could hear his grunts of discomfort every once in awhile. Apparently her assisting me had loosened her chatterbox gene as well and she rattled off information that apparently the tattoo was supposed to have prevented.

"Charlie said that being part of the family created a bond." She continued explaining in her nasal little sing-song voice, "That family don't rat on family, so if we was gonna help him, and get paid, we'd have to join the family. It was easy enough to do. The tat was free and didn't hurt all that much. I was hopin' if I showed Charlie how good I could stand it, he'd do me a butterfly too!"

Nicki finished securing Gary's wrists. I had her move to one side, and I rapidly had her step away so I could inspect her work. I couldn't have done it better. I had Nicki and Gary move over next to the low branch of a massive pine tree.

On the way past their car, I had Nicki remove the long bungee cord that had been wrapped over and over around itself to keep their back hatch of the Toyota closed. I then had her hook the bungee metal loop tightly in the t-shirt rope and then wrap it around through his arms in back. There were a couple of old rusting metal lawn chairs near the tree. I had her pull both over and place them back-to-back. I had Gary climb up in one and I had Nicki climb into the other. The bungee was long enough that it had enough slack to wrap it around the huge tree branch. She did as she was instructed, got down from her chair and assisted Gary in stepping down as well. It was just enough slack pulled tight to bend him over with his arms straight out and slightly up behind him.

I had seen them assume acrobatic poses like this in Circe du Soleil performances hundreds of times.

It looks a lot better when the guy has colored tights on.

It did, however, rendered Gary helpless. I needn't have worried about random acts of bravery on Gary's part. He was a mess. His knees were shaking and he reeked of the pungent smell of fresh urine.

I now had Nicki tear a couple more strips off of what remained of his shirt and part of hers. I had her drag one of the chairs over into my garage shelter and made her sit in it. Hoover assumed guard sentry as I tied her securely to the chair. She was docile enough.

Charlie had apparently not chosen dangerous soldiers for his commune army with these two.

When I was satisfied that Nicki and Gary were immobile, I asked them questions to hopefully clarify my safety level.

"When did you last see Charlie?" I asked leveling the gun at Gary.

"Angela has been here, but we hadn't seen him in weeks till a couple days ago. That ain't unusual. He makes lots of trips down to Mexico and California and on up to Canada. We seen him come in and hook up the trailer a couple days ago and haul out. We figured he was making another run down south."

"Moving drugs?" I asked, knowing the probable answer.

"Well, yeah," said Nicki, "that *is* what Charlie does."

"But not us!" said Gary quickly from his calisthenic spot below the tree branch.

"We just help Charlie with little stuff, we don't sell no drugs."

"When did he get back here with that?" I asked, indicating the gray horse trailer peeking out from behind the house.

"Oh, we heard him drive in real late last night," said Nicki, "so we didn't bother them. We figured he and Angie would have some catching up to do, him being gone so long and all. But he ain't here, his pickup's unhooked from the trailer and he's gone."

Maybe.

I scanned the surrounding woods and started a shelter-to-shelter move toward Charles' house. If he were in the woods watching, one might have assumed he would have taken a shot at Hoover or me by now, but I was cautious in case he had been patient just to draw me out.

No shots were fired, and I made it in through the doorway unscathed. My heart was pounding. I could hear it in my ears.

It was not just from running.

The house looked tidy. Like Charles' room back up Catherine Creek things were very orderly. Obsessive almost. Like his room out of Union, this was a shrine to the 1960's. Posters adorned the wall; an electric guitar leaned against an amplifier in the corner. One wall was a very expensive stereo system. The pre-requisite vinyl LP's of the sixties had been replaced by stacks of CD's, but the music had been replicated to reflect the taste of a man who seemed unable to turn lose of his youth; Canned Heat, Jefferson Airplane, Grateful Dead, Led Zeppelin and Big Brother and the Holding Company.

A stereophonic past brought into the digitally mastered future, by a man who couldn't seem to let go of the good old days.

I could smell the cloying, coppery smell of blood before I was all the way in the kitchen.

Things here were not as orderly. There were overturned kitchen chairs and broken dishes on the floor. A Mr. Coffee maker pot had been overturned and the grounds and coffee had spilled across the counter. They dripped down and mixed with the congealing blood on the floor. There was blood covering the front of one counter and some had puddled under the table.

There had been a struggle and it appeared that although someone put up one hell of a fight, they had probably not been successful.

Was Charlie systematically cleaning up his territory? If so, he must have felt the need to leave here fast, because this was terribly untidy. If he had come back and this had been the last struggle of 'Angela', what had he done with Mary?

I searched the back rooms and turned up no bodies, nor traces of who had been the victim of a nightmare struggle back up here in the woods.

In a back bedroom that had obviously been utilized as an office something again seemed disturbed. The unusual tidiness of Charles was jumbled here, as if he had come for something in a hurry. Charles appeared to be an obsessive keeper of tidy files, files that most criminally inclined felons would never keep for fear of being traced by gumshoes like me, the police, or worse yet, the IRS.

That Charles would not have left this room with empty drawers hanging open and the door of an apparent fireproof safe in the closet gaping wide, unless of course he was running fast and cleaning out his residences as he went. He obviously hadn't figured in enough time to completely empty this house like the one out of Union. Was he planning to do that, but then had something go very wrong with Angela? He would have had to be in a hurry to leave the trailer.

Unless he was coming back for it.

There were definitely things missing. He was on the move and covering tracks and my guess was he had at least one more stop to make.

I eased out the back door and slipped around to the side of the house where the horse trailer had been pulled in tight.

Boxes were piled to the interior roof of the space that was designed to transport up to six horses. If Charles had been using this to run drugs from border to border, it was a clever guise. The Pacific states are rich with horse owners and lovers. Equestrian events, horse shows and 4-H competitions make rigs like this as commonplace as rodeos every summer weekend. Slap a cowboy hat on your head and a bumper sticker professing your love for bull riding and you have the makings of a genuine under-the-radar drug hauler.

I am pretty short, but I managed, by using the trailer's running boards as a step stool, to give the inside of the trailer a fairly in-depth topical search. The trailer had been loaded hastily, so the contents were a loose jumble. I breathed a small sigh of relief; thankful there was no evidence of Mary Milton's murdered corpse in among the cardboard packing boxes and household goods. There were lamps and hastily closed boxes of clothes and dishes. But the trailer's contents did not provide the body that I had almost gritted my teeth and practically held my breath since eastern Oregon expecting to find.

It was not until I stepped down off the running board and onto the ground that I found it.

I tripped over it actually.

The body was under the trailer.

Not completely under, as I had stumbled over the one protruding foot. A small, feminine foot, the nails painted some deep color. It was too dark in the shade of the house to tell what color exactly. I did not want to disturb the crime scene, but I had to know.

I dropped to my knees and peered under the trailer.

CHAPTER TWENTY-FIVE

Like the Cascade Locks waitress had said. She had been a pretty little dark haired thing, skinny as a rail. Angela had undoubtedly been the source of all of the blood in the kitchen. Even given the darkness under the trailer you could tell she was a mess. Because I am possessed of a hopeful nature, I tried her wrist for a pulse.

I was disappointed, of course.

It was hours too late to find Angela's pulse.

I stood and brushed the dirt and pine needles from the knees of my jeans and flipped open my cell phone. *No Service.* I walked back through the house. I was not surprised to find no evidence of a landline phone. I trotted back down to where Gary, bent at an uneven angle, appeared to be bowing politely to his immobile girl friend sitting in front of him in the lawn chair.

They were arguing so loudly that they were almost hissing, and were carrying on so intently that they didn't see me until I was right up beside them. She was accusing him of always getting her into trouble, and he was chastising her for tying his hands so tight.

Knowing I needed information quickly, I assumed my menacing voice and directed it at Gary's sweating forehead. It was interesting to note that even on a cool spring morning, with no clothes on, he was nervous enough to sweat.

"Gary, I am going to ask you once, and only once for some information. I want you to tell me where Charlie goes when he is in Portland. It is important that you tell me correctly the very first time, because if I find out it isn't the truth, someone I am looking out for may die. That would make you an accessory to murder and you and Nicki don't want that hanging over you. Charlie has already killed one person, maybe more. I am still trying to catch up with him so I can find that out. Do you think you can tell me where his Portland house is?"

"Killed? Killed who?" squeaked Nicki from her lawn chair perch.

"Your neighbor Angela is dead, up there."

A small wail escaped from Nicki. Her eyes were wide and she fixed them on Charles house.

I turned back to Gary, he was staring at the house as well and he then looked at me wild-eyed and said,

"We didn't do that, we didn't have nothing to do with that, honest!"

It was time to show a little compassion.

""I want to believe you, Gary. Just give me something to believe."

He breathed an audible, ragged sigh and blurted out, "I took a bunch of dope into a house with him once, out in southeast. I don't know the address, but it was a pink place on the corner of like 160th and Lindsey. He didn't say it was his house, but he sure acted like it was. There wasn't nobody there and he had a key. He just walked right in, got beers for us outta the fridge like he knew they was in there and he got a coat out of the closet and took it when we was leaving."

Gary was so eager to help that his words flew out all in a stream. I didn't think he was a good enough actor to lie, but I decided to test his sincerity. I pulled my gun from the waistband of my jeans. I did not raise it to him, but, holding it in plain sight, I bent over slightly and looked him dead in the eyes.

"Gary", I said in a very calm voice, "I am going to drive to Portland now, and when I get to 160th and Lindsey and find that pink house, I will call and get someone to come untie you. However, if you are not being truthful with me, it will then be way too late for my friend. So, I will then personally turn right around and come back here for you myself. Do you understand the implications of that?"

He was nearly spluttering, "I am telling you the truth, I swear! You'll see, you'll see!"

"Do not try anything stupid." I said to both of them as Hoover and I loped off down the road. It was like telling The Three Stooges not to do anything funny. You got the idea that with Gary and Nicki, stupid undoubtedly just happened.

I could hear them before I was around the first bend. They had resumed the back and forth 'its your fault, no its your fault' argument that I had interrupted.

CHAPTER TWENTY-SIX

My cell was registering a signal by the time I reached the truck. Dan Mickey had given me the direct number of the Multnomah County Sheriff to call upon if I needed help. I placed that call to him. He was out, but I let his office know where to go and what they would find. I left my cell number and let him know I was headed to Portland to search. I suggested they might want to have someone from the Portland Police put a watch on a pink house at 160th and Lindsey. I promised I would be in to make a full report later, for what I realized would be an avalanche of paperwork.

There was a full half an hour to forty-five minutes of travel time between myself - and what might be Charles' next residence. I was counting on the potential of being able to catch up with him in southeast Portland.

For my own peace of mind I had to think that.

I pushed Sam to his and the posted freeway speeds upper limits. There is a crosswind that buffets traffic with some force in the gorge. I was fighting it today. The drive, usually little more than a half hour to forty-five minutes, seemed to take forever.

About ten minutes into the drive three Multnomah County Sheriff's cars shot past, lights flashing, on the opposite side of the freeway. They were headed east. Toward Dodson, I assumed.

It would probably be the first time in their short, misguided lives that Gary and Nicki would actually welcome the arrival of police officers.

No matter what side of the law you dance around on, it is nice to know that good or bad; someone is going to be there to tango with you when you really need a partner.

The sky was cloudless. Several large planes, reducing their altitude in the approach pattern to Portland International, were glinting in the late spring sky.

Tension, stress and adrenaline had made knots in my lower legs and my breakfast omelet was a tight lump in my stomach. I felt like pulling over to be sick along the freeway.

Dead bodies inevitably have that kind of affect on me.

As I drove with one hand, I pulled a Portland street map from the jockey box and located Lindsey. It was not far from a major interchange.

I left the freeway at the closest exit to 160th and made for southeast Lindsey. It was a slightly more populated area than Charles usually chose, although the houses were spaced far enough apart here to offer some privacy. It was a neighborhood that looked like few questions were asked. Maybe sometimes you just don't want to know.

It might have been a housing development designated specifically for body fender repair guys. The front yards and driveways of the houses were littered with project cars. The homes mirrored a bland, sameness. Not a lot of new construction taking place, or the appearance of people rushing out to this particular suburb to invest in future urban expansion. The houses were all probably built in the late 50's and early 60's. Most, having been subjected to years of Portland's almost daily downpours, wore their dull white paint jobs like worn out raincoats.

Except for the house on the corner.

It had, at some time in the past, enjoyed a tenant with a flair to escape the ordinary ticky-tack of the neighborhood. It had been painted the color of a grade school pencil eraser. Now, mellowed by weather and grime to a pale salmon in places, it was indeed 'the pink house on the corner of 160th and Lindsey'.

I knew, as I turned on to the block, that the police had done more than keep an eye on the house.

There were four cruisers; multi-colored light bars flashing, pointed in several directions in the street in front of the Pepto-Bismol pink, corner house.

Two officers had the doors of a dark, silver gray pickup open and were running flashlights under the seats. It appeared to be the same pickup that I had nearly collided with at the end of Charles and Mary's driveway; it also matched the horse trailer in the gorge perfectly.

Two more of Portland's finest stood on the porch talking. Apparently the fireworks, if there had been any, were over.

I parked a couple of blocks away under a trio of trees, by a bridge that crossed a desultory little stream. The morning was warming up. I usually tried to find a cool piece of shade when Hoover was to remain behind. Who knew how these officers would feel about a female private eye, who did not remotely look like a P.I., strolling into a crime scene asking questions, even if I had been the unlikely looking source of the tip that had brought them here. I did not need an over protective blue heeler complicating our introductions.

I strolled casually toward the officers on the porch. I held my license in front of me, so we could avoid their immediate assumption that I was a neighbor coming to chase an ambulance.

We made our introductions and as I assumed, they were grateful for my prior contributions, but were reticent about furnishing me an excess of new information.

It was safe to assume they probably did not have much more than I did.

They did divulge that they had found no one at home. There was evidence that someone had been there recently and that the bathroom had been used to clean up. They had found a pair of jeans, a man's shirt and a woman's blouse that had been saturated with blood stuffed in the bottom of a garbage can.

That was not good news.

There was apparently plenty of other damning drug evidence to justify their taking the place apart, piece by piece, which they were currently in the process of doing.

Eventually, they reluctantly let me in through the front door, realizing I might provide some information that would better connect this house with the other two, or give us all a hint on where to look next.

There was no mistaking the connection.

Charlie always used the same decorator.

Wherever Charlie hung his hat, Haight Ashbury flowered once again. It had been his heyday, and his comfort zone. A time when he could report he had been a big time rock star to a new batch of hippie wanna-be's. It appeared to suit his lifestyle vision of a renegade drug-runner. This house was larger, but similar to the Dodson house; musical posters, instruments, a wall of stereo gear.

Thankfully, this one was missing the blood-drenched kitchen.

Things had been hurriedly disturbed, like in the Dodson house, but it was difficult to tell exactly what had been taken. One thing was easy to spot. There was a similar fireproof safe in the closet of this house, and it, like the one in the gorge, stood, open and empty.

On the move and collecting valuables along the way. I was following a flight pattern, but, unfortunately not quite fast enough.

The lead officer at the scene painstakingly took down everything I told him, but did not seem open or willing to bring me in to their ramped up investigative efforts. I stood about for a bit; frustrated that nothing obvious seemed to leap out at me. I had been so sure that I would have caught up to the whole situation by now, that I was a bit rudderless.

Mostly, I was at a loss as to which direction I should focus next.

I sat on the porch for a bit collecting my thoughts, letting the search efforts of the uniformed officers swirl around me.

I had not checked in with Dan Mickey, so, I headed back to the truck to fetch my cell phone.

Something felt ready to pop out of my brain at me, but things had been racing too fast to let it flow out. I felt like I needed a few moments of complete, meditative quiet. I grabbed my phone from the seat and Hoover opened an eye to assess whether we were ready to go again.

We were not. She closed her eyes and resumed her much needed rest.

I moved around the rear of the truck, went down a slight embankment and plopped down at the side of the small creek.

Like Siddhartha, pondering the mysteries of the universe at the edge of the water, I needed to center my thoughts and decide in which direction I should now proceed.

I had barely dialed in Dan's 541 prefix when I got that direction.

It was then I heard her voice.

CHAPTER TWENTY-SEVEN

"I know you have a gun Cate, so I am watching for any odd movements. As you can see, I have a gun also and I am very good with it. Now, please drop yours into the water in front of you."

She was underneath the small bridge, hidden in the recesses of its rounded cement. Her voice was very quiet, so it really didn't startle me to the degree it should have.

It was also a familiar voice, so my reaction to it was a combination cocktail of relief and horror.

"Eva, are you all right?" I kept my voice low, like hers, still feeling the situation out.

She was squatting on her haunches; elbows rested on her slightly parted knees. It was a solid placement, in order to counter-balance the weight of a rather large caliber pistol.

It was pointed at my head.

"Oh, cut the crap Cate." Her voice grew hard. "I have a police scanner in the truck. I know you know who I am. Good Lord, I *gave* you that. I did not intend you to get this far though. I believe I told you to drop the gun into the water!"

I really didn't want to do that kind of damage to such an excellent weapon. It was the inheritance piece from my investigator mentor, Lew, but I slid it out of my jacket and tossed it down the bank toward the weed-choked water.

"All right then, Mary," my thoughts were spinning, looking for a foothold, "where is Charles?"

"He will eventually surface," she laughed.

It was not a joy laugh. It was mean and devoid of warmth, "or some fisherman above the John Day Dam is going to have a hell of a lot to write home about."

The revelation startled me, but I kept my gaze on her steady and unblinking.

"Did he hurt you, Mary?" I was still speaking with quiet concern. I was unsure whether she was in the midst of some psychotic trauma.

That, coupled with a large gun, was a perilous combination.

"Hurt me? Hurt me?" her voice rose slightly "How stupid are you? That idiotic, womanizing bastard wouldn't dare have hurt me. For heaven's sake, I have carried his drug-addled ass for years. His problem was he just wouldn't quit using the products. That and the fact he couldn't seem to keep his jeans zipped."

"…and you discovered he was keeping Angela?" I added, pieces rapidly tumbling into position.

I didn't care for the 'stupid' remark, but I didn't argue the point. She did have the gun.

"Angela! Lord, at first I thought she was just another one in a long line of his indiscretions. But this time he was actually going to leave me. I knew it. I found out because he kept her letters. He had this compulsion thing about keeping receipts and notes. He couldn't throw *anything* away. Oh, he said *our* time had just run its course, but, not to worry, he was going to split all the cash we had. He wasn't fooling anyone. Mostly he just wanted someone younger. Obviously someone who wasn't tired of his hippy-trippy bullshit."

She was in full, angry release. I said nothing, knowing that sometimes its better if you let a woman scorned really vent.

"I left my *family* for him. I left *everything*. I have done drugs and run drugs. I have prostituted myself and ruined my health in the process. I was going to be an actress. Instead, I spent years wasting my life to keep him happy. All of it so he could act out his big man of the commune fantasy. He surrounded himself with stupid, fawning, juvenile druggies who never seemed to tire of his 'good old days on the communal farm' stories."

"Why did you call me, Mary?"

Her eyes went a shade harder.

"I found some stuff about Angela in one of his jackets, and he had been away for too long. It turns out he had been in a Portland jail, but I thought he had left me for good. I really just wanted him busted. I wanted him to be so very sorry. I wanted you to find him, and then when he claimed I was a willing part of all of it, like I knew he would, I would be gone." She looked at me with a touch of pride; one of her pale eyebrows arched dramatically, "I am very good at *gone*."

"What went wrong, Mary?" I forced myself to remain calm, still hoping she would see me as the confessor private eye she had sent for.

"He came back," she said, reflectively.

Her eyes and her gun were still focused on me, but I could tell she was back in the cabin up Catherine Creek.

"Right after you left, he came back. He was going to leave me for *her*. We argued. He was angry. He figured out that I had called you in. He said I could go look up my rich family and that I didn't need any of the money. He said he wasn't going to take care of me anymore, so, I took care of him."

Her face and voice took on an even harder edge as she continued.

"I calmed him down, said I was sorry, that I would do anything to make him happy. Just like I always had. I convinced him I had made a mistake and we needed to move out quickly. We packed up everything, cleaned the house and then I shot him dead."

Her voice didn't even waver.

"I loaded him into the trailer and I pushed him over the side of a bridge into the Columbia, about halfway down here. Then I came to get the money. It's mine too, you know. Maybe even more mine than his."

"Yes, I suppose it is." I said.

Wonderfully, agreeable me, friend of the working girl.

"Angela?" I asked. The one word seemed sufficient.

"Pfft," she pushed air out between her teeth in an air of dismissal. "That stupid little piece of fluff was going to call the police. That was one of Charles' first rules. We *never* call the police."

Momentarily, another reason I was glad I hadn't taken up the badge.

"Now," she said, her voice changing pitch, "You are going to get a chance to help me after all, in spite of the fact you have been such a nuisance. Since I can't shoot you here because of the noise …"

That is a very loud gun," I agreed.

"…. and I can't just leave you here and drive away, I am going to need you to drive me out of here."

With that she rose up from her crouch and motioned me to get up from the creek bank as well.

"Do not put your hands up, that will draw attention, but keep them out from your body where I can see them." Her voice was dead calm.

She was close enough behind me climbing the small incline, that I felt the gun nudge the back of my rib cage a couple of times.

I was not going to attempt to wrestle the gun away. There was way too much opportunity for error. I was not, however, going to let her get me away somewhere in the truck, where she could shoot me and push me out into some murky body of water. I had just heard her confession. I was a loose end she would have to trim off.

I worked out a quick battle plan.

I made my foot slide a bit in the loose gravel and then I let out a small startled noise. At that moment, I dropped the cell phone I had been clutching in my right hand, down into the gravel at my feet. I knew her eyes would follow that distraction momentarily, and as they did, I saw Hoover's head pop up in the Sam's back window to assess my cry of distress. I raised my left hand as if to steady myself from falling.

It was a natural enough looking reflex, but Hoover saw the palm up signal for 'silence', followed by the palm flat indication for 'get down".

She dropped out of sight.

"Leave it," hissed Mary, referring to the cell phone.

"Not a problem," I replied.

We closed the distance to the truck in about five more steps. We were on the down slope, passenger side.

She then said in that unnervingly calm tone, "Open the passenger side and leave the door open. Get in and slide over very carefully."

I reached up and opened the big red door. Mary was standing slightly back, keeping an eye on me, as well as down the road toward the Christmas tree twinkling of the police lights.

It was a definite step up. This was not a gas friendly, tiny, import truck. This was the Pride of Detroit in 1959. I made it up and in and then arched myself out slightly to give Hoover more room.

As Mary's left-hand fingers wrapped around the inside doorframe, her right hand, clutching the gun, went up to steady herself on the wide open door. Just as her face swung in to bring her body around, she saw the teeth-bared grin of Hoover the Wonder Dog.

It only took a slight movement of my head. Hoover sprang from her crouch, deadly quiet. She knocked Mary sideways. It was an easy effort, as Mary was slightly off balance to begin with, but it was a magnificent canine move, nonetheless.

The gun clattered to the pavement, but did not discharge. I retrieved it. Hoover had Mary on the ground, with just enough teeth pressure on her throat to discourage mobility.

In order to attract the attention of the boys in blue down the way, I decided to run the risk of receiving a citation for discharging a firearm in the city limits.

Besides, you always want to know if the gun that has been trained on you was loaded. I fired Mary's gun into the soft creek embankment.

It was a very loud and loaded gun.

I walked over and released Hoover's sentry. Mary sat up, looking at me and rubbing her neck.

I smiled at her and said with just a hint of smugness,

"*That* is how stupid I am."

THE FINAL CHAPTER

I was correct. The paper work was atrocious.

It was actually more of a police headache than mine, but I did spend much too long in the city answering questions and coming back to testify at the trial. Much longer than I really wanted to.

Every now and again it is good to do that.

It reminds me why I live on the eastside of Oregon.

Give me land lots of land under starry skies above.

Mary's elderly father arrived, with the housekeeper-bodyguard, Mrs. Elder in tow. He was understandably grateful to find his only child still alive. He brought in the finest legal assistance big money can indulge.

Charles, whose remains were eventually located near a small island in the Columbia, unable to defend or protest, was thoroughly villanized by the Milton's legal team, as well as the media. Then again, they had plenty to work with. They were provided hours of airtime and pages worth of speculations and theories to wallow about with.

Sex, drugs and rock and roll. The Holy Grail and the backbone of the media sales trinity.

However, once you get the bad guy, or gal in this case, things generally tend to start wrapping themselves up.

Mary was eventually found to be legally unhinged. The trial was a circus production number; 'Barnum and Bailey do San Francisco'.

Gen X hippies camped on the courthouse steps with a wide assortment of banners and causes begging pitiful attention.

Every woman's organization on earth with some kind of an axe to sharpen, tried to use Mary's situation as their whetstone. They weighed in heavily each evening on the chats, demanding that she was a victim and should be set free.

That all died down when the prosecution revealed that Mary really had, all along, been the brains behind the operation.

A handful of former 'Helpers' turned up for their 15 minutes of notoriety. It became almost chic to have been a part of the whole 'Mothers' movement. For awhile people were claiming 'they knew them when', when in fact most of the wanna-be camp followers weren't even a gleam in their parent's pot-shot eyes in the 1960's.

The bonafide Helpers, genuine ex-members who did show up to spill their guts, painted a picture of a woman that most people would rather not display as their *cause du jour* poster child.

Bad Queen Mary, The Evil Empress of Illegal Smiles.

Mother's Helpers, a truly formidable entity in the 60's and 70's, had, in actuality, dissolved in the late '70's. They had continued to live in the glory days of Charles' mind, but most people can only take so many drugs, risk lifelong incarceration, sleep in so many crash houses and eat so many bulger burgers. Pretty soon you have to start thinking about how nice it would feel to drive a BMW and lose the three-window panel delivery truck.

The core of Mother's original members, save for Charles and Mary, went off to become part of the establishment they had rallied so feverishly against. Some fell obediently into the spouse, two children, nine to five workday grind. Some went to jail. Others were able to tidy up their personal histories enough to start businesses and even run for public office.

I ponder sometimes, watching the evening news, the curiosity of how a generation, who most vehemently protested the government and it's intrusion into their lives, ended up getting themselves elected and then themselves creating layer upon layer of government agencies to control peoples lives.

I guess you file that under 'don't do as I do, do as I say'.

Mary had indeed left La Grande on her own and run back to Charles and the Helper's family. So much for Daddy's claim that she couldn't or wouldn't hurt her mother's feelings. She had digested the taste of wild California freedom and decided she was hungry for more.

How 'ya gonna keep 'em crackin' the books, after they've danced nude, on LSD, in Golden Gate Park?

She found herself wildly bored when she had been forcibly taken home and removed from the action.

Daddy said no more hippies. Mary said bye, bye daddy.

She had faded into the tie-dyed camouflage that was the '60's, apparently never looking back with any familial regret.

When it came right down to it, Mary had been more than just a great actress. She was leadership material from the start.

She quickly took up the reins in her and Charles' burgeoning drug business. In the end, he was as much a follower as his motley posse. She managed to keep herself out of the limelight, and jail, by using Charles as the front man. She was a runaway to begin with and she stayed hidden.

Time did little to change her shadow life.

Charles did the grunt work; she ordered him around and spent the ill-gotten gains.

Like most actors, she really just wanted to direct.

She had, over the years, divided her time between Berkley, California and Eugene, Oregon. It was easiest for counter culture advocates to blend in those two communities, but she got a particular charge out of periodically returning to La Grande, the scene of her disappearance, where she had left her youth and family.

In the end, the whole freedom thing didn't go all that well for her.

Mary's legal eagles tried to paint a maudlin picture of an innocent aspiring thespian, lured by evil drug dealers from the safety of her ivy-covered confines. That she had willingly run away from home to rejoin her captors was nearly overlooked.

Nearly.

Drug dealers or users aside, the jury just couldn't get past a floating husband and his very dead paramour.

She was placed in a secure prison-mental hospital for well-to-do loonies. I personally think anyone who kills their fellow man, or woman, for reasons outside preservation doesn't need the justice system to certify them. Whether or not it justifies a good defense; who am I to say?

The courts assured the world that Mary would have years to pay for her crime behind those hospital bars.

I remain unconvinced.

As twisty and drug addled as she had become, she is one who is truly born to the stage.

I regularly picture her convincing a parole board, long before her time served, that 'she now knew the error of her ways, and that even though he was her man and he was doin' her wrong, nice, substance-free girls from good homes just aren't killers.'

Carl, nee Stevie Waters, the delivery boy, was merely another of Charles' 'posse' of young users. He had a small history with the local Union police department. He was one of those kids that too many little infractions as a kid growing up start looking like trouble brewing when you total them up on a police rap sheet. Truancy, petty thefts, underage drinking parties and poor peer selection begin to look serious; like someone you might be dealing with housing permanently as an adult.

He was a perfect character for Mary's revenge charade. He was flattered by his association with Charles and was malleable enough for Mary to enlist as a gopher.

He believed her, but then many of us did.

When you consider the irony and her flair for the dramatic, she probably would have made a pretty good actress.

Stevie, frightened into sobriety by his brief brush with the acid queen, was actually one person who benefited by his association with Mary. The realization that he too could have been floating alongside Charles in the mighty Columbia brought him the reality check he needed. The last I heard he was clean, sober, newly married and attending Blue Mountain Community College in Pendleton with an eye on a career in welding.

Gary and Nicki did a little time in jail, but provided enough vital information to the police to keep their sentences light. That pair and Stevie were a fair representation of Charles' dream team; a loose conglomeration of hop heads and small time druggies who assisted Charles' transport of drugs from the Mexican to Canadian border. They did the local work of spreading the supply of 'poison-ala-carte' to children and adults along the established drug highways. There will always be human mules to packhorse contraband, but Charles' personal use of his products eventually destroyed his ability judge good horseflesh. His empire of communal helper-bees rapidly dissolved with his passing.

Dr. Milton, Mary's elderly father, apparently forgiving and grateful for my part in Mary's capture, sent along a *very* nice check. I accepted.

A girl does incur expenses.

As soon as things returned to what I consider normal, I bought Hoover and I a brand new camper canopy for the back of Sam. A lovely, sturdy tip-out model made locally by Nash Trailers.

Sam looked absolutely magnificent.

I packed my new camping palace with more food and kibble than we could eat, more books than I could read and headed off into the eastern Oregon hills vowing to stay gone till I was through being gone.

It had been way too long since I had taken real time off. Every so often people ought to get away to where people aren't. It is a meditative exercise in human sensory deprivation; a getting to know yourself game that is a valuable inner-awareness tool.

Hoover just likes to have all of my attention for herself. Being able to roam for hours in the woods is, to her, Doggie Club Med.

Sheriff Dan, my Peterson landlords and my small batch of intimate friends waved me off, wished me well and smiled indulgently.

Vacation or not, they knew I couldn't avoid the lure of a challenging case for too long.

-END-

COLLEEN MACLEOD